THE ANGEL TRIALS

DARK WORLD: THE ANGEL TRIALS 1

MICHELLE MADOW

DREAMSCAPE PUBLISHING

RAVEN

THE LAST WAY I'd ever imagined spending my twenty-first birthday was by working the register at my mom's new age store—Tarotology—below our Venice Beach apartment.

If I hadn't traipsed off on a solo backpack trip around Europe without telling anyone—and without returning until after the semester began—I'd be getting ready for a night out with my friends right now.

Instead, I was grounded. And I still didn't even know *why* I'd gone to Europe.

Yet, I'd done it.

The memories of the trip were hazy—like I was watching someone else go off on the adventure instead of me—but they were there.

According to the spiritual psychologist my mom had

dragged me to, I'd suffered a break of the heart and mind. I was now taking a variety of herbal medicines every day and sleeping with crystal healing wands next to my bed to "mend the break."

It was ridiculous. Herbs, crystals, and all that stuff were pseudo-science. But my mom had threatened to stop paying for my college if I didn't cooperate, so I had to go along with the program. Sure, I could have taken out a student loan, but getting into massive debt when I didn't need to would have been an unwise decision.

So, here I was. I just needed to get through the next few weeks. Then the summer semester would start, and my life could finally return to normal.

"Excuse me?" a customer asked—a short lady who looked to be in her forties. "Can you help me select a tarot deck?"

"Of course." I pasted on a customer-friendly smile and walked with her to the tarot stand. The stand was large and in the center of the shop, since tarot was the store's specialty. "They're all right here," I said. "Look through the cards in the sample decks, and select the deck that calls to you."

Her brows knit in confusion. "How do I know which one is calling to me?" she asked.

I wished I could roll my eyes and tell her to just choose the one she thought had the prettiest pictures.

But obviously that wasn't an option, as it would ruin the "mysticism" of the experience.

"Handle the cards—shuffle them, and look at the images on each one," I said, maintaining a practiced serene smile. "Try to sense a personal connection between yourself and the cards. Once you do, bring the deck up to the front so I can ring you up and give you your free tarot reading."

"Perfect." She smiled and reached for one of the decks. "Thanks for your help."

"No problem." I returned to the register and glanced at my watch, glad to see that there was half an hour left until closing.

The lady eventually selected a tarot deck, and I gave her the promised free reading. As always, a few tactical questions allowed me to generically relate the cards to her life and impress her with my "psychic abilities."

"Can you give yourself a reading, too?" she asked once I was done. "I'm curious how else the cards can be interpreted."

"All right," I agreed. "I'll give myself a simple one card draw."

I shuffled the cards and picked one from the deck, placing it on the table between us.

A skeleton in black armor riding a white horse stared up at me.

Death.

The lady scrunched her nose. "That's grim," she said.

"Not always." I sat straighter, forcing perkiness into my tone. "The cards are metaphors—they shouldn't be taken literally. The Death card doesn't mean that someone close to me will die. It refers to transformation or change. The death of an old way of life so a new one can arise."

"Interesting," she said, although I could see she was still spooked. "Pick another card."

"It was a one card draw," I said. "I'm not supposed to pick another."

"I'm superstitious, and I don't like the look of that card." She leaned forward and gave me a small smile, as if egging me on. "One more can't hurt, right?"

"Fine." My mom wouldn't be happy, but what she didn't know wouldn't hurt her.

I selected a second card and placed it face-up on the table.

It was the Tower—a card with a burning tower in the center, lightning striking above, and people falling out of the windows.

"That one doesn't look good, either," the lady said.

"Like Death, the Tower represents change," I told her. "Usually in the form of sudden disruption, conflict, or upheaval."

"Well, then." She took a deep breath and clasped her hands together. "It looks like you've got something big to prepare for, doesn't it?"

"Looks like it," I agreed, since to someone who believed in all of this, that *would* be what the cards were saying. "Oh—and I recommend grabbing a quartz crystal from the basket." I motioned to the basket full of quartzes in front of the register. "They're only five dollars each, and placing a quartz on top of your tarot deck while you're not using it will cleanse its energy for future readings."

"Wonderful." She reached into the basket and placed a quartz next to her deck. "Definitely add that on."

"My pleasure." I smiled and slid her credit card through the machine.

And cheers to the up-sell.

2

RAVEN

I'D JUST FINISHED CLOSING up the shop and was about to head upstairs when someone banged on the front door.

I took a deep breath in preparation to face whatever entitled person thought the shop should remain open for a bit longer just because they saw someone inside.

Instead, I saw the smiling faces of my three closest friends—Kaitlin, Tiffany, and Amy. They were all dressed up, looking ready for a night out on the town.

I rushed over to the door and unlocked it, opening it but not letting them inside. "What are you guys doing here?" I asked, despite being happy to see them.

"What kind of friends would we be if we forgot your twenty-first birthday?" Kaitlin said with a sly grin. "We're here to take you out."

I threw my head back and laughed. "Fat chance of

that happening," I said once I'd recovered. "You know I'm under house arrest until the end of the semester."

"About that…" Tiffany's eyes twinkled with mischief. "Your mom's the one who reached out to us. It was her idea to give you the night off."

"What?" My mouth dropped open in shock. "You've got to be kidding me. This isn't some April Fools' prank, is it?"

Having a birthday on April First was the *worst*. I hated being the butt of pranks, but when your birthday's on a day devoted to pranks, everyone takes it as an invitation to make you the center of them.

"Not a prank." Amy placed her hands on her hips, looking offended. "Don't you think we know you better than that?"

"Of course," I said, since it was true. The three of them had been there with me since our freshman year of college. They were the sisters I'd never had.

"So are you coming or what?" Kaitlin asked.

"I need to thank my mom… and I need to change." I motioned to the flowing white new age shirt I was wearing, since my mom insisted I wear her hippie clothes while working at the shop. "Wait down here. I'll be back in ten minutes tops."

I rushed up the steps and into the apartment, thrilled with the prospect of freedom for the night.

My mom was already waiting at the kitchen table, a small gift bag in front of her. "I guess your friends arrived on time?" she asked with a smile.

"It's true then?" I held my breath in anticipation. "You're cutting me loose for the night?"

"You only turn twenty-one once," she said with a flourish of her wrist, the many bangles she wore clanking together with the movement. "I couldn't take this experience away from you, no matter how much trouble you got yourself into this winter."

"Thank you." I rushed over to her and enveloped her in a hug.

"You're welcome," she said once the hug was broken. "And the night of freedom isn't the only thing I'm giving you for your birthday." She reached for the bag and handed it to me, her eyes glimmering with a fine sheen of tears. "This is for you."

Curious to discover why the present was making her so emotional, I sat down and dug in. A jewelry box was inside. I opened it, revealing a beautiful lapis lazuli charm necklace.

It was the one my mom always wore.

She never took it off, but it was absent from her neck now.

"You're giving this to me?" Guilt filled my chest at

the thought of accepting the present, since the necklace meant so much to her.

"I know you're skeptical about the power of crystals," she said.

I said nothing, since she was right, and we both knew it.

"As you know, lapis lazuli helps open the window to the soul," she continued. "I bought this necklace for myself when I turned twenty-one. The crystal helped me get more in tune with my abilities, strengthening them into what they are today. I hope that wearing it will do the same for you."

"But I don't have any abilities," I said gently, placing the jewelry box down on the table in front of me. "You know that."

"I know you *think* that," she said. "But I've been telling you since you returned from Europe that something big is happening in the world—a shift from light to darkness."

It took all of my self-control not to heave a sigh.

My mom had been preaching doomsday mumbo-jumbo for weeks. I'd been hoping she'd drop it, but she was growing more paranoid each day.

I was getting concerned about her. She'd always been eccentric, but the doomsday stuff was a whole new level of crazy.

"Something's coming, Raven." Her eyes were fervent as she held her gaze with mine. "Darkness looms on the horizon. Last night I did a tarot spread for you—it seemed appropriate, on the eve of such an important birthday—and the cards made the upcoming change clear."

"What cards did you select?" I asked.

"I thought you had no faith in the cards?" She sat back and raised an eyebrow in challenge.

"Humor me."

She nodded, looking thrilled to share her findings. "I did a three card spread," she said. "Regarding your past, present, and future."

"And?" Anxiety brewed in my stomach as I waited for her to spit it out. Which was silly, since I didn't even believe in this stuff.

"I pulled Death, the Tower, and the Chariot."

3

RAVEN

I FROZE, my heart pounding. What were the chances of her drawing *both* of the cards I'd pulled for myself earlier? And in the same order?

Statistically, it wasn't impossible.

But it was certainly improbable.

"All three cards have to do with change," she said, apparently sensing my unspoken desire to hear her interpretation. "Death in the past was likely referring to your European getaway. It was so unlike you—a definite change from your normal behavior."

I nodded, since the trip being unlike me was something we both agreed on.

"The Tower in the present is not only worrying, but it confirms my intuition of sudden change or upheaval," she said. "Then there's the general interpretation of the card—that of demons being released from ancient hiding places." She shuddered, clearly disturbed just from talking about it. "I can't help but feel like it relates to the darkness I've been sensing in the world. Perhaps it even needs to be taken literally."

"I don't know." I shifted uncomfortably, not liking where she was going with this. "Aren't the cards always metaphors?"

"They're *usually* metaphors," she said. "There are occasional exceptions."

"But isn't that an extreme interpretation?" I hoped she didn't *literally* think demons had been released upon the world.

If she did, I'd have to get her psychological help. She wasn't going to like it. But because I loved her and wanted her to be healthy, I'd do it if these delusions continued getting worse.

"Moving on," she said with a wave of her hand. "Your future card—the Chariot—brings hope to the spread. An adventurous journey awaits you. I've always interpreted the Chariot as a card of triumph, but the future is never set in stone. I don't know what your journey will be, but as long as you follow the advice attached to the Chariot card—to be prepared for the upcoming changes and to be receptive of new people who come into your life— you'll have the best chance of achieving that triumph.

And always remember—*you* are the charioteer of your own life. Embrace that power, rejoice in it, and don't let anyone take that power away from you. Understand?"

She studied me intensely, silence descending upon us. And while I wanted to chalk it up to coincidence, the eeriness that had crept over my spine when she'd mentioned the first two cards was still there.

"This is the most thoughtful I've ever seen you after a reading." She steeped her fingers together, looking as patient as ever. "Is there something you want to tell me?"

I waited a few seconds, eventually figuring I had nothing to lose by being honest.

"After giving a customer her free reading today, she asked me to pick a card of my own," I said.

"And?"

"I chose Death."

"The card of your past." Her eyes lit up at the connection. "The same one I drew for you last night."

"There's more," I continued. "The customer didn't like the card, so she asked me to pick another. I did, and I picked—"

"The Tower," she interrupted.

"How did you know?"

"I can tell by your expression," she said. "You never take the cards seriously, but you know as well as I that the probability of the same draw is slim."

"Yeah." I wrapped my arms around myself, trying to organize my spinning thoughts. Because while choosing the same cards was improbable, there was a logical explanation for what might have happened.

My mom could have been listening during the reading I did with the customer, and was completely making it up that she'd done a draw for me last night.

"What happened next?" She leaned forward, her eyes wild. "Did you pick a third card?"

"Nope." I shrugged off my unease, satisfied with my conclusion that she was pulling one over on me. The only thing keeping me from calling her out was that I didn't want her to change her mind about un-grounding me for the night so I could celebrate my birthday. "I changed the subject by convincing her to buy a quartz crystal, and that was the end of that."

"Wait here." She stood up suddenly, her chair screeching across the floor, and hurried to her room. She re-emerged with her tarot deck and handed it to me. "Let's do another one card draw," she said. "Then I'll let you go, I promise."

I shuffled a few times for show. Once finished, I handed the cards to her, and she laid them out in a spread.

"Pick one card," she said. "Think about the two

previous cards you drew—Death and the Tower—and about how they relate to your future."

I reached forward and selected a card from the spread, ready to get this over with so I could go out with my friends. Ten minutes had already passed—they were probably getting antsy and wondering what I was doing.

I placed the card face up, and…

It was the Chariot.

"What?" I stared at her in shock, because there was no way that was a coincidence. "Were you listening to me down there? Did you make me pick this card?"

That must have been it. She could have gone to the stock room, opened 78 decks, pulled the Chariot card from each of them, and made a fake deck of all Chariot cards.

As far as April Fools' pranks went, I'd have to give her credit for that one.

"How could I *make* you pick a card?" She chuckled. "You shuffled and chose the card on your own."

I didn't bother explaining my theory. Instead, I collected the cards back into a pile and looked through them.

Each card was different.

The deck hadn't been tampered with.

"It's not possible." I put the deck back down and

pointed to the Chariot card staring up at me. "How'd you get me to pick that?"

"I didn't 'get' you to pick anything," she said. "You chose the Chariot because an upcoming journey is your destiny." She reached for the lapis lazuli necklace—*her* necklace that she'd gifted to me—and placed it in my hand. "I don't know what this journey will entail, but the Tower card in the present position shows that it will come about swiftly and forcefully. That's why I'm asking you to wear this necklace. The stone will awaken your destiny and purpose, and it will help you tap into your abilities. You'll need them for whatever's coming next."

"But I don't *have* any abilities," I repeated.

"You're my daughter," she said. "You have abilities. Magic runs in our blood."

"I know, I know." I held a hand up, since the last thing I needed was to hear yet another rendition of our "magical" family history.

"Please, Raven," she begged. "I'm not comfortable with you going out tonight without this necklace. Wear it, so I know you'll be safe."

"Fine," I gave in, clasping the necklace around my neck. The stone rested gently over my skin, and it almost felt like it was pulsing with warmth. "And thank you for letting me go out tonight," I added. "I really appreciate it."

"Anytime." Her eyes gleamed with sadness, like she couldn't believe her little girl was growing up. "Have fun tonight. And be safe. I love you."

"Love you too."

I gave her a quick kiss on the cheek before hurrying to my room to change and heading downstairs to join my friends.

4

NOAH

NOTHING COMPARED to the freedom of running through the forest in my wolf form, but riding my motorcycle down the curves of the Hollywood Hills sure did come close.

Sage Montgomery rode beside me, as she had throughout my mission. It was a good thing I'd met Sage— well, a good thing that Sage had found *me* in a dingy underground LA shifter bar—when I'd arrived to California.

Sage and I had connected instantly—she was like the sister I'd never had. I would have been a clueless mess trying to navigate human society without her help.

Now, we pulled up to the gate in front of the modern Beverly Hills mansion owned by the most powerful circle of witches in LA and entered the guest code into the keypad. The camera zeroed in on me, and the light turned green, the gate swinging open.

We parked in the drive, and Sage hopped off her bike, swinging her long dark hair behind her. "Have I thanked you yet for convincing me to buy the motorcycles?" she asked with a grin.

"Only a handful of times." I smirked, running a hand over the leather seat of my bike.

It hadn't taken *that* much convincing to get Sage to charge the bikes to the Montgomery pack's credit card. I didn't know much about human money, but from what Sage had told me of the Montgomery account, they had more of it than they could ever need.

Enough that buying fake papers, identification, and everything else I needed to pass as someone from civilized society had been done in the blink of an eye.

"I can't believe we're halfway done with our hunt," she said, and I instinctively reached into my pocket, feeling the five demon teeth that were in there—teeth from the demons I'd hunted and killed. "It won't be the same here once you're gone."

"You sure you don't want to come with me?" I asked. "Avalon's looking for trained fighters, so you definitely fit the bill."

I did a good job hunting demons, but I'd be lying if I

didn't admit that there had been one or two times when Sage had saved my ass.

There was a reason why wolves hunted in groups— or at *least* in pairs. We were always better together than alone.

"As tempting as that sounds, I can't leave my pack," she said. "They're part of me. I'd never be able to live with myself if I left them forever."

"I get it," I said, since I did.

Leaving my pack had been one of the hardest decisions I'd ever made.

It was the right decision—I could do far more at Avalon than I could by staying home—but I'd be lying if I said there still weren't days when I wondered what my life would have been like if I'd stayed.

"I'll keep doing my part here in LA," Sage said with a smile. "If Avalon ever needs a contact out here, I'm your girl."

"Don't you forget it," I said. "And maybe once I'm in Avalon, I'll be able to get you a slicer of your own."

"That would be amazing." She eyed up the dagger inside my open jacket, hunger flaring in her gaze.

The Earth Angel Annika herself had given me the dagger when she'd told me that I needed to bring her the teeth of ten demons I'd killed for admission to Avalon.

An angel had dipped the dagger in heavenly water, which gave it the ability to slay demons.

Technically, the dagger was called a "heavenly dagger," but I thought "slicer" had a better ring to it.

"No promises," I said, since I had no idea what awaited me in Avalon. "Anyway, let's head in before the witches think we're loitering." I strolled over to the massive glass door. "We've still got five demons to hunt."

5

NOAH

AMBER—THE leader of the LA witch circle—opened the door and ushered us inside the mansion that looked more like a modern art museum than a home. As usual, she was wearing yoga pants and an oversized sweatshirt, her blonde hair up in a messy bun. Only her floral supernatural scent gave any hint that she was a powerful witch.

Amber wasn't the only witch I smelled inside—there were others as well. But unlike Amber's fresh scent, they smelled sickly sweet, like syrup.

I'd asked Sage about them after the first time she'd taken me here, and she'd explained that while Amber practiced light magic, most of her circle practiced dark magic. That syrupy scent was the smell of a dark witch.

Luckily, the other witches stayed upstairs. Amber

was the only witch of her circle who dealt with customers.

"I take it Tijuana was a success?" she asked as she led the way to the spell room.

At least, I thought of it as a spell room. Amber called it the *apothecary*.

"Would we be here if it wasn't?" I asked.

"Perhaps," she said. "You could need our help for a mission gone wrong. But you're both looking rather confident, so I'm assuming that wasn't the case."

"You assumed correct." Sage grinned. "This one gave us quite the chase, but we got her, just like we've gotten the rest of them."

"Glad to hear it." Amber opened the door to the apothecary, motioning for us to enter first.

Automatic lights turned on the moment we stepped inside, which was good since the apothecary was the only room in the house without windows. There was an empty table in the center, and cabinets along the walls displayed potions, crystals, and herbs. The only other door in the room was small and padlocked. I assumed it was a storage room.

"I take it you're here for the usual?" Amber asked once the main door was shut.

"Yep." I removed my slicer from its sheath and placed it on the table. "A demon locator spell."

She retrieved her pendulum hanging on the wall and an atlas shelved nearby, placing them on the table next to the slicer. "You know the deal," she said, looking at Sage. "I trust you both, but payment first."

"Of course." Sage reached into her bag and handed over her shiny black credit card.

Amber swiped the card through a device attached to her phone and handed it back to Sage. "Now time for the fun part." Her eyes gleamed as she opened the atlas to a map of the Western USA. Once the map was positioned, she retrieved four different colored candles, placed them on all four points of the map, and lit them with a match. Each candle smelled like a different element. Earth was north, fire south, air east, and water west.

When all four candles were burning steadily, she picked up the pendulum and my slicer. As she'd explained this first time I'd seen her do this spell, this was so she could *channel* the essence of what we were seeking—in this case, demon blood similar to the blood that had been on my dagger—and connect that energy with the pendulum to locate it.

She zeroed in on the map, and her breathing slowed into long, steady breaths—like she was meditating. The room smelled like it blossomed with flowers as her magic burst to life.

I held my breath as I waited for the pendulum to move. If it didn't, we'd come back every day until it did. We wouldn't be charged again until she located the next demon, but sometimes we had a longer wait between hunts than others.

Just when I thought we'd be coming back tomorrow, the pendulum started swinging with a life of its own. It pulled Amber's hand away from the center of the map, toward California.

I didn't speak—I didn't want to interrupt Amber's concentration—but my veins pulsed with excitement. The closer this demon was to home, the sooner we could kill it.

The pendulum finally stopped swinging right over one of the largest city dots on the state.

"LA." Amber's eyes widened as she said the name of our home base. "There's a city map in the front of the atlas." She spoke quickly, the bitter scent seeping from her pores revealing her fear. "Pull it out and place it under the pendulum."

Sage was quick to do as instructed.

With the new map underneath it, the pendulum started swinging again. I'd seen this happen before— Sage and I had consulted witches at each city we'd visited to pinpoint the location of the demon we were hunting—but there was something different about watching it happen against a map of the city I'd been calling home for the past few weeks.

I didn't like the thought of one of those creatures on my home turf.

Amber moved her hand with the pendulum until it stopped swinging, pinpointing the location of our next hunt.

The writing on the map was gibberish to me—a fact I didn't share with others if I could avoid it—so Sage said the name of our destination out loud.

The Santa Monica Pier.

6

RAVEN

"Seriously?" I asked when Kaitlin pulled into the parking lot. "We're going to the Pier?"

"It'll be fun!" she said. "We can play tourists in our own city. But it's your birthday, so if you don't like the idea we can go somewhere else..."

"No," I said. "You're right—it's been ages since I've been to the Pier. Let's do it."

"Good." Tiffany smiled and glanced at her watch. "Because we have reservations at the Mexican restaurant, and we're almost late."

"And after dinner we can go on the rides!" Amy squealed, clapping her hands together like a little kid.

"That sounds perfect," I said. It really did—especially since I'd never been fond of clubs, which was where a lot of people went for their twenty-first birthdays. Now that I was over the corny tourist aspect of coming out to the Pier, I had to admit it was a fun idea. "Thanks, guys."

We entered under the lit up sign, meandering around gawking tourists who kept stopping to take pictures with the rides in the background.

"We should take a picture." I took out my phone and flipped it onto camera mode. "After all, you only turn twenty-one once." I raised the phone to take a selfie and snapped a few, although it was hard to get all four of us *plus* the background in the frame.

"Let's get someone to take it for us." Kaitlin took the phone from my hand and turned to two people passing by—a guy and a girl decked out in leather.

They looked ready for a motorcycle convention—not for the Santa Monica Pier on a spring night. They were also both jaw-droppingly gorgeous. I'd always considered preppy guys to be my type, but something about the way this guy's shaggy brown hair framed his dark, intense eyes took my breath away.

"Excuse me," Kaitlin said to him, apparently unfazed by his incredible good looks. "Would you mind taking a picture of us?"

He glanced at the phone like it was poisonous and sneered. "I'm no good with those things." He didn't even bother to look at us—it was like he thought we were vermin. "Find someone else." He tugged on the girl's arm, and she shrugged in apology before following him away.

"Some people are so rude," I muttered. "How hard is it to take a picture?"

His back straightened, and he turned around to glare at me. I would have thought he'd heard me, but he was far enough away that that was impossible.

We quickly found someone else to take our picture. Once checking to make sure we all looked good in it, we continued along the Pier. The restaurant was all the way at the end, so we got to pass by all the carnival booths and rides. We were already discussing which ones we wanted to try.

"Raven!" someone called from a booth off to the side. "Raven Danvers!"

I looked over to see who was calling my name, expecting it to be someone from school. Instead, I saw a tanned, exotic-looking teen girl who was wearing sunglasses, despite the fact that the sun was nearly done setting. She stood inside a humble blue psychic booth called "Rosella's." She appeared to be working there.

She looked familiar, so I waved, figuring she was a customer I'd helped at the store.

"Do you want a palm reading?" she asked. "Complimentary, of course."

"Thanks, but we have dinner reservations and we're

already running late," I said with what I hoped was a kind smile, pointing my thumb toward the restaurant. "Maybe once we're done!"

I wasn't coming back once we were done, but there was no need to insult her. She was just trying to be nice since we worked in the same industry.

"As you wish." She removed her sunglasses and stared at me with eyes so vacant that I shuddered.

It was only upon reaching the restaurant that I realized why her eyes looked like that.

She was blind.

But if she was blind, how had she known to call out my name while I was passing by?

7

RAVEN

MY FRIENDS ORDERED a round of shots the moment we sat down at the table.

"IDs?" the waiter asked with a raise of his eyebrow.

I handed mine over and held my breath. Even though I was legal now, ordering drinks at a restaurant was still making me feel like I was doing something wrong. I supposed being twenty-one would take some getting used to.

"Happy birthday." He handed it back with a smile. "You get a complimentary drink of your choice. What'll it be?"

"Smirnoff Ice," I said on instinct.

"Coming right up." He headed off to grab it.

"Now that you're twenty-one, you need to find a

drink that *isn't* known for catering to the underage crowd," Kaitlin said with a laugh.

"Hey!" I held out my hands in defense, pretending to be offended. "Don't trash talk my Smirnoff Ice."

The waiter returned quickly with my Smirnoff Ice and the tequila shots. He took our orders, and I got the least vegan thing on the menu—a ground beef burrito with extra cheese melted on top. My mom only kept vegan food in the house, so I delighted in eating meat and dairy at every other opportune moment.

"Things are getting wild tonight." Amy grinned devilishly at the shots and rubbed her hands together. She reached for hers and held it up, and we all followed her lead.

"To Raven's twenty-first birthday!" Kaitlin said.

"And to her night of freedom!" Tiffany added.

"Cheers to that." I smiled at them, and we all clicked our drinks together before downing the shots. It took a lot of self control not to gag as the liquor burned its way down my throat, but I forced it down, my eyes watering as I finished the last of it.

Luckily, a swig of deliciously sweet Smirnoff Ice was just the remedy to flush out the taste of tequila.

"So," Kaitlin said, turning to me in excitement. "Tell us about your European adventure!"

"Yeah," Tiffany agreed. "What made you go in the first place?"

"And why haven't you posted any pictures online yet?" Amy asked.

They all leaned forward, watching me eagerly.

I lowered my eyes, knowing my answers were bound to disappoint them.

"I'm not sure why I went," I said softly. "It's weird. I mean, I always wanted to do some traveling at some point, but not like that. Not so unplanned."

I shuddered at the thought of going anywhere without a plan—*especially* to a foreign country. Yet, I'd gone. I did the whole backpacking thing, taking the train from place to place, and going on tours recommended by other people in my hostels. And I did it with cash that I *sort of* remembered saving up, since there was no record of the trip on my credit card.

I thought I'd enjoyed the trip, but it was all hazy now. Like a dream instead of real life.

I hadn't talked about it with my friends because I didn't want them to think I was losing it. Who goes on a trip but doesn't remember *why*, or if they even had fun while there?

And while my mom and I didn't see eye to eye on much, worrying her by disappearing without telling her where I was going made me feel sick every time I thought about it. She'd thought I'd been kidnapped. Or worse—killed.

It was why I hadn't argued with her decision to ground me. Yes, it was ridiculous for a twenty year old to be grounded, but it was also unacceptable for *anyone* to act the way I had.

I deserved the punishment.

"Going without a plan *was* very unlike you." Kaitlin smiled, and I could tell she was trying to lighten the conversation. "Heaven forbid that anyone should ever ruin one of Raven's plans. You had each semester of classes planned up to your senior year—starting from back when you were a freshman!"

"Of course I did!" I laughed and ran my fingers along the crystal on my neck, glad to be back on more familiar territory. "I need all the required courses to apply to medical school. You have no idea how hard it is to get into the right labs."

Although of course, now that I was behind a semester, that plan had gotten messed up too. Why had I ever thought it was a good idea to gamble my future on such a whim?

I sat back and frowned, taking another swig of my drink as if it could wash my worries away.

"What about pictures?" Amy leaned forward, apparently oblivious to how I didn't want to discuss Europe.

She was the smallest of the four of us, so I assumed the shot had gone to her head. "Don't tell us you went to Europe and took *no* pictures?"

"My phone broke on the journey home." I shrugged. "I lost all my pictures with it."

"Oh." She frowned. "Bummer."

Luckily the waiter came with our food before the inquisition could continue, and the topic of Europe was forgotten as we feasted on our meals. The girls were happy to tell me about all their latest guy drama, and I was more than happy to listen so I'd no longer be the center of attention.

After clearing our plates, the waiter returned with another Smirnoff Ice. "A gift from the gentleman in the plaid shirt at the bar," he said as he placed the drink in front of me, tilting his head toward the guy he was referring to.

Heat rushed to my cheeks. I'd never had a guy send a drink over to me before. That was something that happened in movies—not to me.

I wasn't sure what to do, so I looked over at the guy and raised my drink up in thanks before taking a sip.

He was cute. I wasn't sure how old he was, but he looked around my age, or maybe a few years older. With his tanned skin and long blond hair, I guessed he was here on vacation to catch some waves.

"You should go talk to him," Tiffany said.

"Just walk up to him?" I balked. "And say what?"

"Thank him for the drink," Amy said. "He bought it for you, so he wants you to go talk to him. It's the perfect in."

"Hmm." I didn't look in his direction, since I didn't want him to know we were talking about him. "He's cute, but tonight we came out for my birthday. I want to hang out with the three of you—not with a tourist who's only in town temporarily."

"How do you know he's a tourist?" Kaitlin asked.

"We're on the Santa Monica Pier," I deadpanned. "*Everyone* here is a tourist."

She nodded, apparently not going to bother arguing with that one.

"He's still looking at you." Amy leaned forward and smiled like a giddy schoolgirl.

"Just go talk to him for a few minutes," Tiffany said. "Find out if he's local or not. We'll still be here when you're done."

"Fine," I gave in, since he *was* cute. "If you insist."

I stood up and turned around, my breath catching in my chest when my eyes met his. He angled his body toward me and gave me a small smile—a clear indicator that my friends were right. He wanted me to go talk to him.

I straightened and took a deep breath in, holding my drink tighter for comfort. I wasn't sure why I was so nervous. It wasn't like this was the first time I'd ever talked to a guy.

But something about him felt... different.

One of my friends nudged me—I didn't look to see which one—and I got the hint. I couldn't keep standing there staring at him.

So I flipped my hair over my shoulder, and as confidently as I could, walked in his direction.

8

RAVEN

"For a moment I thought you weren't going to come over here." He smiled when I reached him—a relaxed smile that I was sure put everyone at ease. Now that I was closer, I saw that his eyes were as blue as the Pacific Ocean itself.

"I'm out with my friends for my birthday." I motioned to where they sat around the table, trying—and failing—to look like they weren't watching us. "But since you were so kind to buy me a drink, I figured the least I could do was come over here and thank you personally."

"Happy birthday." He raised his drink—some kind of fancy liquor that I'd expect an old businessman to be drinking—and raised an eyebrow. "What's your name?"

"Raven," I said.

"Nice to meet you, Raven." He clinked his drink with mine. "I'm Eli."

I took a sip of my drink and fiddled with my necklace, unable to ignore the nudging feeling in my mind telling me to go back and rejoin my friends. The feeling made no sense, since Eli was being a perfect gentleman, but it was there.

"Would you care to join me?" He motioned to the empty seat next to him at the bar.

I glanced over my shoulder at my friends. The moment I looked over, they all looked away, pretending to be engrossed in conversation.

"I understand that you're here to spend time with your friends, so I won't keep you from them for long," he said, and I turned back to look at him, captivated in his ocean blue eyes once more. "I promise."

His immediate understanding of my feelings put me slightly more at ease.

"Whether or not I join you depends on how you answer one important question," I said, holding my gaze with his.

"Intriguing." He smirked—apparently I'd piqued his interest. "What's your question?"

"Are you a tourist, or do you live here?"

If he was a tourist, I'd go back with my friends. If he lived here, it seemed fair enough to give him a chance.

"And why does everything rest on this question?" He was quick to respond.

"Because if you're a tourist, you'll be gone in a few days," I said. "If you're from here, then..." I shrugged, not wanting to come off as one of those girls who was always planning ahead—even though I *was* one of those girls who was always planning ahead. "Then who knows?"

"I'm not a tourist," he said. "I'm new in town."

"Oh?" I raised an eyebrow and slid into the seat next to him, since that was the deal I'd made with myself before asking the question. "What brings you to LA?"

"A job." He took a sip of his drink, not looking like he wanted to elaborate.

"What kind of job?" I couldn't resist asking. Curiosity was practically embedded in my DNA.

"That's top secret." He swirled his drink, his eyes locked on mine. "Let's just say that I... hunt for things. I'm a collector of sorts."

"Okay..." I twisted at my necklace. He was looking at me like *I* was one of those things he was hunting, and discomfort descended upon me again.

Maybe I should have gone back to my friends earlier —or not have approached him at all.

"Tell me about your necklace." He reached for my hand to stop my fidgeting. "It's a very unique piece."

I pulled my hand away from his, reaching for my drink to take a sip. Eli's mention of the necklace reminded me of my "Plan B" when it came to trying to make a guy not interested anymore—saying a bunch of strange stuff to make him think I was a complete weirdo, so he'd be *glad* when I walked away.

The necklace gave me the perfect opportunity to do just that.

"This necklace isn't actually mine." I reached for it again, gazing at him like I was preparing to tell him a deep, dark secret. "It's my mom's. She gave it to me for protection... because she's a witch."

"A witch?" Eli raised an eyebrow, apparently intrigued.

That wasn't the reaction I was hoping for.

"What makes her think that?" he prodded.

"One of my ancestors was killed in the European witch trials." I spoke slowly, like I was telling a scary story around a campfire. "But the people who were killed weren't innocent like history says. They were actual, real life witches. My ancestor was a witch... and so is my mom."

"What about you?" He leaned forward, his eyes gleaming with anticipation. "Are *you* a witch?"

He was getting pretty excited about this witch stuff. Maybe I needed to tone it down a bit.

"No," I said, since it was the truth. "But my mom isn't convinced. That's why she wants me to wear her special crystal necklace. She thinks it'll bring out my powers." I widened my eyes, positive that I looked like an absolute crazy person.

"Is it working?" He focused on the necklace, nearly salivating as he looked at it.

I pulled away, reaching for the necklace to stop him from trying to touch it. "Of course not." I laughed in an attempt to throw him off. "I'm not a witch, and neither is my mom, no matter how much she wants to think otherwise. Witches don't exist."

"You'd be surprised," he said, and I resisted the urge to roll my eyes.

"Despite being constantly surrounded by people who believe the paranormal exists, I've yet to be surprised." I stood up and grabbed my drink, flipping my hair over my shoulder. "Anyway, it was nice chatting, and thanks again for the drink, but it's time I head back to my friends."

I turned around and headed back to the table, not wanting to give him the chance to ask me another question. I felt a little bad for blowing him off, but at the same time... something about Eli gave me the creeps.

And it didn't take a witch or a psychic to know that when a creepy guy was hitting on you, it was best to walk away as quickly as possible.

9

RAVEN

My FRIENDS and I hung out at the table with another round of drinks, although I felt like Eli was watching me the entire time. I was relieved when he finally left the restaurant. Once he was gone, I got up to use the restroom.

The room swayed a bit when I stood. I guessed that was to be expected after all the drinks. I barely managed to walk straight toward the hall in the back where the bathrooms were located, but I made it.

I definitely needed to have a glass or two of water once I got back to the table.

After washing my hands, I paused in front of the mirror to steady myself and freshen up. My long, wavy red hair was a mess, and my makeup was smudged around my eyes since I'd had it on since opening the store.

I tried wiping under my eyes with a paper towel and running my fingers through my hair to soften it up, but it was hopeless. I supposed my grunge look would have to do.

I'd just stepped out of the bathroom when a big hand wrapped around my mouth, and a sharp metal object pressed against my neck. "Scream and I'll slit your throat," the guy whispered hotly in my ear.

My heart leaped in terror. Was I being mugged?

I eyed the back hallway, praying someone would turn the corner toward the restrooms. No such luck. I tried to scream despite his warning, but it was muffled against his hand.

Not again, I thought as he forced me through the back door, into the alley behind the restaurant.

Why had I thought that? I'd never been mugged or taken against my will before.

But it was happening now. And the sooner I got away, the better my chance of survival.

I needed to fight.

I squirmed and struggled, but it was hopeless. This guy was *strong*. My attempts to escape didn't bother him in the slightest. I wasn't even sure if he'd *noticed*.

So I rammed the stiletto of my boot straight into the top of his foot.

He flinched, but his hold on me didn't loosen. "Bitch," he grunted. "Don't try that again."

I struggled again anyway, but his hold was so tight that it was like trying to push through concrete.

"Eligos," another man said from behind us. "I see you've brought me a present."

My captor twisted us around, bringing me face to face with a fit, middle-aged man in jeans and a zipped leather jacket standing next to an overflowing dumpster. I could have sworn that his eyes glowed red for a moment, but it had to have been the lighting.

"This one's weak," my captor said. Now that he wasn't whispering, I recognized his voice. It was Eli. "But her necklace will lead us to a stronger one."

The middle-aged man walked closer to me. I struggled again, and he eyed me up, like he was getting pleasure from my fear. Once there was only a foot between us, he reached forward and ripped my mom's necklace right off me.

He barely glanced at it before shoving it into his pocket.

"She's definitely weak," he said. "But it can't hurt to add her to the collection. Plus, she's not bad on the eyes, is she?" He chuckled, lust burning in his gaze as he ran his finger down my cheek.

I would have spit at him if Eli's hand hadn't been covering my mouth.

"She's a bitch," Eli said. "I wouldn't expect to get much fun out of her."

Horror dawned on me as I realized what was going on. They were traffickers kidnapping me for a sex ring.

I refused to let that be my fate. I needed to get away from them.

But how?

We were in a back alley, they were two strong men, and Eli had a knife to my throat. With his hand covering my mouth, I couldn't even scream.

I'd never felt so helpless in my life.

But there had to be *something* I could do. After all, I'd rather have him slit my throat than be forced to do whatever they were kidnapping me for.

So I rammed my elbows into his stomach, hoping to knock the wind out of him so he'd let me go. From there, I'd run.

Pain reverberated through my arms, like I'd smacked my elbows into a wall. I would have collapsed from sheer agony if Eli's arms hadn't been around me.

"They always think they can fight." The older man shook his head. "Their entire species is pathetic."

It shouldn't have been surprising that a trafficker was a sexist prick, but I narrowed my eyes at him anyway.

"She'll learn who her true boss is soon enough." Eli's tongue snaked in and out of my ear, and I swallowed down the bile that rushed up my throat. "They all will."

Suddenly, two people appeared from around the corner, running so quickly that they were a blur.

Once they stopped, I recognized them instantly—the leather-clad couple who had refused to take our picture at the entrance of the Pier.

The guy freed me from Eli's grasp in seconds, and he shoved me toward his female companion.

She caught me before I tumbled to the ground, holding me steady. "Stand back," she said.

I didn't have time to process what was happening before she let go of me and ran toward the older man, her knife raised in the air.

He shimmered and disappeared.

She ran straight through the place where he'd been standing, stopping and looking around in confusion.

I blinked, sure I must not have seen that correctly. But apparently, I had.

The man was gone.

And the girl's male companion—the guy who had

saved me—had Eli pinned against the wall. They struggled, but despite Eli's strength, my savior was stronger.

He raised his knife and shoved it into Eli's heart.

Eli disintegrated on the spot. He was there one second, and gone the next. Like he'd never existed at all.

This was insane. The first man disappearing... Eli disintegrating... it wasn't possible. I had to be hallucinating.

Eli must have slipped something into my drink while we'd been chatting at the bar.

Maybe the two who had saved me were helping me, or maybe they were members of a rival gang and were going to kidnap me themselves.

But I didn't plan on finding out. Right now, all that mattered was getting to safety.

So I rushed for the door and flung it open, hurrying into the restaurant without stopping to look behind me.

10

NOAH

THE DEMON DISINTEGRATED, and I turned around, ready to fight the other one that Sage had run to attack.

Sage was there, her eyes wild and frantic, but the demon was gone. I'd have thought she'd killed him, but since I was the only one of us with a slicer, that was impossible.

"Where'd he go?" I gazed around the alley, my knife raised in preparation.

"He disappeared," she said, breathless. "Or teleported. Like some kind of witch."

"But that wasn't a witch," I stated the obvious. "It was a demon."

We stared at each other, and I knew we were thinking the same thing. This was the sixth demon we'd hunted—well, seven, since there were two of them tonight—and we'd never seen a demon teleport.

Either they were gaining powers, or that wasn't an ordinary demon.

"At least the girl's safe." I glanced at the door she'd scurried back inside of. Her human mind had likely already rationalized what she'd seen, like most of them did when witnessing a supernatural event. "I wonder what those demons wanted with her?"

"They were hunting her." Sage flipped her knife around and slid it back into her boot. "The question is— why her?"

"No idea." I shrugged. "Maybe cause she was hot?"

"Seriously?" She rolled her eyes, although I could tell by the way she chuckled that she was amused. "You managed to check out some human girl while kicking demon ass?"

"She was the same girl who asked us to take her picture with her friends back at the entrance," I said, turning my focus back to the demon ash by my feet. As always, all that remained were its teeth.

I reached down and picked one up—it was yellowed and pointed, like all the demon teeth I'd come across on my hunts—and dropped it in my pocket.

Six down, four to go.

"There must have been *some* reason why the demons chose her," Sage mused.

"The reason why demons are hunting specific humans is something for Annika and her army to figure out at Avalon," I said, checking my pocket to make sure all six teeth were there. They were. "All I need to worry about is getting those final four demon teeth so I can *get* to Avalon. And if demons can now teleport, that's gonna make this mission a hell of a lot harder."

"So what's the plan?" Sage asked.

"We go to the only person who might have an answer —and who might be able to get us a potion or spell to counteract the teleporting."

"Amber." Sage said it as a statement, not a question.

"You got it." I wiped my knife on my jeans and slid it back inside my jacket. "It looks like the witch hasn't seen the last of us today."

11

AMBER

MY SISTER BELLA teleported into the living room with a dirty, chained man by her side. She looked ravishing in a tight red dress with lipstick to match, her dark wavy hair flowing down her back.

The man was more than twice her size, but he was on his knees, staring up at her as he quivered in terror.

"Bella?" Our other sister Whitney ran down the stairs, Evangeline hot on her tails.

Other than me, Whitney was the only other light witch in our circle. Bella, Evangeline, and Doreen all practiced dark magic. Doreen was the only one not home right now, as she was out on a hunt.

"This scumbag was the leader of a drug ring in Venezuela and is responsible for orchestrating over a hundred murders." Bella smirked, her hand still gripping his shoulder. "He led us on quite the exhilarating chase."

"Well, get him out of the living room and into the dungeon." I crossed my arms and looked down at him in disgust. "All that blood and dirt on his knees is messing up the new rug."

Bella tugged on his chain, dragging the filthy drug lord into the apothecary.

He followed her without putting up a fight—my sisters always shot their finds with complacent potion to make them easier to handle. The apothecary and the dungeon below were blocked from teleportation spells, so we couldn't transport the prisoners straight into their cells. It would have been cleaner if we could, but security was a priority.

As dark witches, Bella, Evangeline, and Doreen needed to use the blood of those they'd killed to perform their strongest spells. Those spells and potions were the most expensive ones we sold—meaning they kept us living in our accustomed style.

Which was why we'd teamed up with the vampires of the Tower—the vampire kingdom in South America —and they helped us hunt down the most dangerous human criminals on their continent. Those criminals then got locked in our dungeon so our dark witches could kill them to perform their magic.

We paid the vampires for their assistance in the hunts, and then we charged even *more* money to the clients who purchased our dark magic spells and potions.

It was a win-win. Especially since we took dangerous criminals off the streets in the process, stopping them from killing who knows how many innocent humans.

I grabbed a bottle of champagne, and Whitney gathered the glasses. We always made a toast whenever Bella or Doreen brought in a new criminal. They had the strongest teleportation magic, so they went out on the hunts. Whitney, Evangeline, and I weren't skilled at teleporting, but we were exceptionally talented with difficult spells and potions.

Together, the five of us were a kickass team.

Once Bella had returned from the apothecary—sans the dirty murdering scumbag since he was now locked up in the dungeon—I popped the cork, holding the bottle up in victory.

Suddenly, a demon clad in leather appeared in our foyer. His eyes glowed red, and he smiled, showing off his pointed, yellowing teeth.

Terror rushed through me, and the bottle slid from my hand, falling to the rug. Champagne flowed all over the floor. I didn't bother picking it up, instead just staring at the demon in fear.

His magic reeked of smoke and fire. This was the first demon I'd ever seen, so it was also the first time I'd smelled the demonic magical signature.

"How did you get in here?" Bella stepped up—she was always the most daring of us—and placed her hands on her hips. "We have a boundary spell around this house."

I focused on strengthening the spell, looking at Whitney to do the same. From the intensity shining in her eyes, I could tell she was already on it.

Boundary spells were light magic, so we were the only two in our circle who upheld it. It didn't take much effort, since it only had to surround our property, and the two of us were strong enough to easily maintain a spell to keep out all humans and supernaturals.

We'd thought we were safe against demons... but apparently we were wrong.

"Your spell is strong," he said. "But not strong enough to keep out a greater demon like myself."

I swallowed and stepped back, terror going all the way into my bones.

But he still hadn't attacked. Which I assumed meant he didn't want us dead.

I could work with that. I *had* to work with that. Because my sisters and I had nothing on a greater demon. The only creature that could kill a demon was a Nephilim, and the only one of those in known existence had turned into an angel and was living on the mystical island of Avalon. Apparently she was trying to turn humans into Nephilim to build a demon fighting army, but no one outside of Avalon knew if she'd been successful yet.

"Why did you come here?" I looked the demon straight in the eyes, trying to sound as cool and collected as possible.

He reached into his pocket and pulled out a necklace with a lapis lazuli pendant. "I need a scrying spell done to determine the location of this necklace's owner," he said.

I stared at him in disbelief. This greater demon had come to us... as a client?

That was the last thing I'd expected. But since we couldn't fight him, what else could we do but cooperate?

"Very well," I said, and then I quoted him the price for the spell. The price I'd quoted was double what we normally charged for a simple scrying spell, but if we were going to be forced to work with a greater demon, we'd better be paid handsomely for it.

He teleported over to Whitney and thrust a knife into her stomach before I could blink.

"No!" I screamed, running to my sister to help her.

The demon pushed me away with enough force to propel me across the room. I grunted as my back and elbows collided with the marble floor, staring up at the demon with undisguised hatred in my eyes.

Bella and Evangeline rushed to me, and they each grabbed onto one of my arms, pulling me back up to stand.

I looked upon my fallen sister to assess the damage. The demon had removed the weapon, and Whitney had fallen to the floor. She was using her hands to apply pressure to the wound, but the blood was leaving her body fast, forming a puddle on the floor around her.

Witches didn't have the accelerated healing of vampires and shifters. We relied on potions for healing, but the potions weren't perfect. They couldn't heal fatal wounds.

I prayed her wound wasn't fatal.

"You'll perform the spell for free." The demon snarled. "Or one of you will be next." He looked at Bella and Evangeline when he said the final part, and I didn't doubt his words. This creature was evil incarnate, and he'd do whatever it took to get what he wanted.

Scrying spells were light magic, which meant with Whitney indisposed, I was the only one able to perform the requested spell.

I needed to get my act together. If I didn't, Bella and Evangeline would face the demon's wrath because of it.

"Come with me into the apothecary." My voice was devoid of emotion, and I spoke to the demon like he were any other client. "I can easily perform a scrying spell to find the location of the necklace's owner. For free, of course."

"That's more like it." He smirked and swung the necklace around like it was some kind of weapon. "Please, lead the way."

12

AMBER

I PERFORMED the scrying spell using the same method as I had with Noah and Sage earlier. It was difficult to focus with the demon's red eyes watching me, but I managed.

My sisters' lives depended on it.

Once I zeroed in on the location, I wrote down the address—a new age store in Venice Beach called Tarotology—and handed the slip of paper to the demon.

"I don't think I need to tell you what will happen if I find out that this is the incorrect address?" he asked.

"It's the correct address," I said. "I promise."

He studied me, and apparently he believed me, because he teleported out without so much as a thank you.

He left the necklace behind.

I rushed to the shelves, pulled out every healing potion I could carry, and hurried out of the apothecary.

Bella and Evangeline sat next to Whitney, holding her hands. Her eyes were closed—she'd fallen asleep. But while I could smell Bella and Evangeline's syrupy dark magic signatures, Whitney's magical scent of flowers no longer lingered in the room.

I cradled the potions in my arms, staring at my sisters hopelessly.

Witches had spells and potions for nearly everything, but we couldn't bring back the dead.

"She's gone," Bella said, even though I knew already. "But it wasn't in vain."

"What do you mean?" My voice cracked when I spoke. "She was murdered by that…" I paused, searching my mind for an adequate term for the greater demon. "That *monster*. How is that not in vain?"

"The greater demon mortally injured her," Evangeline said. "Whitney knew you wouldn't be able to return with the potions in time, and that even if you did, it wouldn't work. So she used her Final Spell to strengthen the boundary around the property—to make it strong enough to keep out greater demons."

Tears rolled down my cheeks at the realization of my sister's sacrifice. The Final Spell was the strongest spell a witch could cast—but it involved he or she using their life force to cast it.

Whitney had used her Final Spell to protect us.

"She didn't need to do that." I sniffed. "I might have gotten back in time with the healing potions…"

Bella walked toward me and wrapped her arms around me in a hug. It was a bit difficult since I was still holding the vials of potions, but she managed. "They wouldn't have worked," she said, and when she pulled away, she stared at me with eyes as fierce as a warrior. "But now we're safe in this house. Which means we have to do everything we can from here to help stop the demons."

"We will." I looked at my fallen sister's pale corpse, and fury, determination, and most importantly, *purpose* flowed through my veins as I thought about what was coming next. "I won't rest until the last of the demons are dead."

13

RAVEN

I PUSHED past all the tables and chairs, causing a scene as I hurried to the table where my friends waited for me. My entire body shook with terror—I wasn't sure how I was managing to walk—but somehow, I made it back to them.

"Raven?" Kaitlin stood up, her eyes flashing with worry as she reached for my arms to steady me. "What happened?"

Just at that moment, a line of waiters paraded out of the kitchen with a cake lit up with a candle, grinning and singing "Happy Birthday."

It was like a scene from a nightmare. All these people smiling at me, and all I could do was replay the last few horrifying moments in that alley in my mind.

The song ended, and Kaitlin leaned down to blow

out the candle. "Raven's not feeling well," she told the waiters. "Can you give us some space, please?"

"Is there anything we can get you?" Our main waiter looked at me in concern. "Some water, perhaps?"

"I need to get out of here," I mumbled, glad when Kaitlin led me by the elbows out of the restaurant. Tiffany followed close behind, and I heard Amy call out to the waiters about getting a check.

Once we were outside, I leaned against the front wall of the building and took a deep breath to steady myself. Tiffany handed me a glass of water—she must have taken it from our table—and I chugged it down gratefully.

By some miracle, I was safe. I was *alive*.

"Raven?" Kaitlin repeated my name. Her voice wavered—I could tell she was scared, too. "What happened back there?"

Amy joined us, and the three of them watched me in concern.

"I think he drugged me," I somehow managed to say.

"He?" Amy's eyebrows knitted in confusion. "Who?"

"Eli," I said. "The guy who bought me a drink. The one I talked to at the bar. When I was coming out of the bathroom, he grabbed me and held a knife to my throat and pulled me back behind the restaurant where this other man was waiting..." I sniffed, wiping away the tears that I only now realized were rolling down my cheeks.

"Oh my God." Amy's mouth rounded in horror. "How'd you get away?"

"We need to call the police." Tiffany whipped out her phone, ready to dial.

"Wait," I said. "I just want to go home."

"But this needs to be reported," she said. "Those men need to be caught."

"They're not there anymore." I swallowed, unsure how to tell them the rest of what had happened. "Two other people came and saved me."

"Where are they?" Amy looked around at the people milling about the Pier. "Why aren't they with you?"

"I don't know," I said. "I ran back inside the first moment I could."

"Smart," Kaitlin said. "You did the right thing getting out of there." Suddenly her arms were around me in a huge hug. "I'm so glad you're okay," she said. "I can't imagine how terrifying that must have been."

I nodded, although I felt like the true horror of my experience hadn't even had a chance to sink in yet.

"Are you sure you don't want me to call the police?" Tiffany asked. "They need to know what happened…"

"Can we do that tomorrow?" I asked. "If we call the police now, we'll have to stay here for who knows how long, and I don't think I can handle that right now. I just want to go home." My lower lip trembled—I felt on the verge of a breakdown if we stayed any longer.

"All right." Kaitlin gave a warning look to Tiffany and linked her arm in mine, leading me down the Pier. "Let's get out of here."

We were passing Rosella's booth when the teen who'd offered me the free palm reading earlier saw me.

"Raven Danvers!" she screamed my name.

I walked faster, ignoring her. Kaitlin kept my pace, her arm still linked in mine. After what had just happened, I was in no mood to be heckled again.

But the girl ran up to us, blocking our path and staring at us through her dark sunglasses. I started to walk around her, but she reached for my arm that wasn't linked with Kaitlin's, stopping me.

"Don't touch me!" I tried to pull my arm away, but her grip was strong. And there was something strange about her hand—there was no heat coming off her skin. It was like she was a robot or something.

She removed her sunglasses, revealing her milky, unseeing eyes. "The turning point has just been reached." She stared at me, despite being clearly blind.

"Be ready for a shock when you get home. But remember that I—Rosella—have the answers. My door is always open. When you're ready, I'll be waiting here to guide you."

She slid her sunglasses back on, let go of my arm, and scurried back to her booth.

I stared at where she'd stood, anger and confusion swirling in my veins. After what I'd just been through, the last thing I needed was a crazy boardwalk psychic trying to reel me into her store. That was the icing on the seriously awful cake that had been my twenty-first birthday.

"Who was that?" Kaitlin glanced at the booth, looking seriously spooked.

"I don't know." I marched toward the exit, pulling her with me. "And I don't care. I just want to go home."

14

NOAH

It took longer than usual for Amber to buzz us through the gate.

Once inside the house, I was assaulted with the strong, flowery smell of witch blood.

"What happened here?" I looked to where the scent was coming from—a puddle of blood off to the side of the room. There was also a broken bottle of champagne on the rug.

Whatever had happened, it didn't look good.

Amber quickly filled us in on everything the demon had done. "Bella and Evangeline are with Whitney in the apothecary right now," she said, her eyes brimming with tears. "They're preparing her body for burial."

"I'm so sorry for your loss." Sage walked up to Amber and gave her a hug.

Amber collapsed into the embrace. Sage wasn't usually the touchy-feely type, but I was glad she was with me, because I would have had no idea what to say to Amber if I'd come alone.

I'd suffered so much loss recently that I suspected I was becoming numb to it.

"Thank you." Amber sniffed and pulled away.

"That demon is why we're here now." I was quick to get to the point, continuing on to tell her about what had happened in the alley.

"He's a monster." Rage burned in her eyes as she stared at the bloodstained floor where he'd murdered her sister.

"He can also teleport," I said. "I've been hunting demons for a few weeks now, and I've never come across one who could do that."

"That's because he's not a regular demon—he's a *greater* demon," she said. "You're lucky he teleported away. If he hadn't..." She let the sentence hang, allowing us to draw our own conclusions.

"Since only Nephilim can kill greater demons, we wouldn't have been able to kill him if we'd tried," I said. "He could have destroyed us. So why did he leave?"

"Maybe he thought we *were* Nephilim." Sage held her hand up, pointing to the black ring around her finger.

I had a matching ring—it had been one of the first

spells Amber and her circle had done for us when they'd learned of our hunt. The rings cloaked our scent, which allowed us to sneak up on demons unaware.

The greater demon had seen our speed, so he knew we were supernatural. But the rings stopped him from knowing what *kind* of supernatural. He must not have wanted to take the chance that we were Nephilim there to slay him, so he'd flashed out.

"That must be it," I said. "But if we run into a greater demon again, we can't count on being lucky twice. We need a way to defend against them."

"I'll look into possible spells or potions tonight," Amber said. "But whatever I come up with, I won't have it ready until tomorrow. And it'll likely be dark magic, so it won't be cheap."

"We can come back tomorrow," Sage said. "And the cost is no matter."

"I figured as much," Amber said. "I hope we can find something that can help you. That demon..." Her eyes went blank, and she shuddered, as if replaying what had happened with him in her mind. "I don't know what the Earth Angel is doing on Avalon, but she *has* to figure out a way to create new Nephilim. It's the only way to stop these monsters. If she can't do it..."

"Annika's a force to be reckoned with," I said. "If anyone can build an army of Nephilim, it's her."

"I hope so." From the darkness in Amber's tone, I could tell she was doubtful.

"I'm sorry again about Whitney," Sage said to Amber, reaching for my arm and nudging me toward the door. "We'll leave you with your sisters now to grieve."

"Wait." I pulled away from Sage, focusing on Amber. "You did a scrying spell for the demon. Where did you send him?"

"We can't go after him." Sage looked at me like I'd gone crazy.

"Why not?" I asked. "You were the one who was curious about what the demons were hunting."

"Because we can't defend ourselves against greater demons," she said slowly. "You know that. We'd be walking to our deaths."

"Greater demons can *teleport*," I reminded her. "I'm sure he's already gotten what he needed and left by now. If he hasn't, we can hide out and check it out once he's gone. Our rings will hide our scent. He won't even know we're there."

"I thought you didn't care about what the demons were hunting?" Sage asked. "You just wanted to get the rest of your demon teeth and get to Avalon?"

"The more information I have, the more indispensable I'll be once I get to Avalon." I shrugged. "Plus, if we know what the demons want, it could help us in our hunt. So?" I turned back to Amber, ready to set off. "Where did he go?"

"A new age store in Venice Beach," she said, reciting the address. "It's called Tarotology."

"Thanks." Sage whipped out her credit card. "How much do we owe for the information?"

"Nothing." Amber shook her head, her eyes empty.

Sage froze, looking shocked. It was unheard of for the witches to do anything—even supply simple information—without compensation. This was clearly a first.

"I insist." Sage held the card out. "The Montgomery pack prefers paying to owing favors."

Amber looked at the card but didn't take it. "That demon took my sister from me," she said, her voice laced with venom. "You figuring out what's at that shop that he wanted badly enough to take Whitney's life to find it is all the payment I need."

"We're on it." I backed toward the door, itching to get moving now that we had a lead. "And thanks for the tip."

Without further delay, Sage and I left the mansion, revved up our bikes, and sped off toward Venice Beach.

15

RAVEN

IT WAS ONLY a ten minute car ride from the Pier to Taro-tology. I spent the entire drive staring out the window, thinking about what had happened in the alley.

I'd told my friends it had been an attempted kidnapping. I *still* believed that.

But I couldn't forget the inhuman speed of my rescuers, the way the older guy had disappeared into thin air, and how my savior had stabbed Eli and turned him into a pile of ash.

It was the drugs, I reminded myself. Eli *must* have slipped something in my drink that had made me hallucinate.

Otherwise... I was either suffering from a psychotic delusion, or something supernatural had happened in that alley.

It had to have been drugs. Except I didn't *feel* like I'd been drugged. I'd never been drugged before, so I supposed I had no way to tell if I'd been drugged or not, but I felt the same way as when I'd had one beer too many.

It was one of the reasons why I hadn't wanted Tiffany to call the police. The police would test me for drugs, and I feared I'd come back clean.

Which would mean I was suffering from a psychotic break.

It was exactly what I'd feared since the jaunt to Europe. I'd thought I was getting better, but now... that apparently wasn't the case.

It was time to make an appointment with a real psychiatrist. Not one of those new age organic doctors my mom was sending me to who'd give me herbal supplements and crystal wands to try purifying my aura, but a trained professional who could get to the bottom of what I was experiencing and help me get better through actual *science*.

Tomorrow, that was exactly what I planned to do.

THE TRAFFIC WAS INSANE—LIKE always—but eventually Kaitlin pulled up to the back of the shop. Even though it was only five feet from the car to the door, my friends insisted on walking with me.

After what had happened tonight, a hollow pit formed in my stomach at the idea of walking anywhere by myself. Especially at night.

My friends made me promise I'd call them tomorrow. Then I locked up and hurried upstairs to the apartment, ready to change into my pajamas and tell my mom everything. It would be such a relief to get it off my chest.

I stopped dead in my tracks when I entered the kitchen.

A chair was overturned on the floor, and a half-eaten plate of pasta was on the table. The stovetop was still on with leftover dinner simmering in a pot, and the television blared with the local news. The tarot cards remained where they'd been earlier, so the Chariot card was still face-up on the table.

"Mom?" I dropped my bag on the table and hurried to her room.

Her lights were off, the room was empty. She wasn't in the bathroom, either. I called for her again and looked for her in my room—I didn't know *why* she would be in my room, but it was the only other room in the apartment left for me to check.

She wasn't there.

I would have thought she'd gone out, but she wouldn't have left the kitchen in such disarray, and her car was still in the lot behind the building.

I hurried to my bag and took out my phone to call her. We were walking distance to a lot of places—maybe she'd gone somewhere and hadn't thought to let me know. She had no reason to think I'd come home early on the night of my twenty-first birthday.

I turned off the television, tapped her name on my speed dial, and held the phone up to my ear.

Her phone rang behind me.

I turned around. Sure enough, her phone was on the kitchen island, lighting up with my call. I ended the call and slid the phone into my back pocket, dread seeping into my bones.

The overturned kitchen, the food left on the stove, the phone left behind... it was all adding up to look like my mom had been taken.

I leaned against the wall, my breaths shallow, and tried to get ahold of myself. How could someone have gotten in here? The back door had been locked when I'd gotten home, the balcony door was shut, and the front—the entrance for the store—had an alarm system.

Maybe she'd gone downstairs to the store to check on something and left her phone up here? After what had happened to me tonight, I was automatically jumping to the worst conclusion by thinking she'd been taken, but I was probably panicking for nothing. She could be doing a last minute inventory check.

I flicked on the light near the steps and hurried downstairs to find her.

But if she was down here, wouldn't she have turned on the lights?

"Mom?" I pulled aside the curtain that led to the front, looking around the empty store in panic. Next, I checked the back room. Nothing.

That was it. She wasn't here. I was calling the police.

I ran upstairs and heard two vehicles pull into the back.

"This is it," someone said—a male. "He's been here. I can smell him."

"What would a demon want with a human-run store?" the second voice—a female—said.

"No clue," the man said. "But I doubt he left anyone behind, so let's take a look and find out for ourselves."

I hurried to my bedroom and peered through the blinds.

Two motorcycles were parked next to my mom's car. The people who'd been speaking—who I presumed had come on the bikes—were nowhere in sight.

Thumping noises came from the balcony—like

they'd climbed up. But that was impossible. It was too high to climb, especially that quickly.

But there was jiggling on the outside, and the door started to open. My heart jumped into my throat. I wouldn't be able to get out of the apartment without them seeing me.

I was trapped.

I closed the door to my room and glanced around for something to use to protect myself. It was a situation like this where owning a gun would have come in handy, but my mom was *way* too anti weapons to have ever considered it. Instead, I grabbed the biggest healing crystal wand on my nightstand and hid in the closet. The crystal was half a foot tall, as wide as a broomstick, and it had a pointed tip, so it could double as a weapon.

I hoped. Which would have to be enough, since it was all I had right now.

Securing the crystal in one hand, I grabbed my phone out of my back pocket with the other and dialed 911.

They picked up after the first ring. "911, what's your emergency?" a calm woman asked from the other side of the line.

"Someone's in my house," I whispered, not wanting to risk them hearing me. "I got home and my mom was gone and now I think whoever took her is trying to take me too."

"Where do you live?" she asked, remaining perfectly calm.

I quickly gave her my address. "It's an apartment," I added. "Above a store called Tarotology."

"The police will be there in ten minutes," she said. "Are you in a safe place?"

I glanced around the closet and at the crystal wand in my other hand, unsure how to answer her question. "I'm hiding in a—"

I was midway through speaking when the door to my room creaked open. Footsteps sounded through my room. I stayed as quiet as possible, not wanting to give away my location, and raised the crystal wand higher.

It wasn't much, but I refused to go down without a fight.

"Miss?" the voice on the other end of the line asked. "Are you still there?"

The footsteps got closer and closer until they were right in front of the closet. Then they stopped.

I held my breath—whoever was inside was standing on the other side of the door.

The door opened, and with as much strength as I could muster, I arced the crystal back and rammed the tip of it straight into the intruder's flesh.

16

RAVEN

SHE CURSED, and I bolted to the door without stopping
to look at her.

But the man who had saved me in the alley was
standing in the doorway, blocking my path. I ran
straight into him, and he wrapped an arm around me to
keep me still. He used his other hand to swipe my phone
from my hand.

He glanced down at the screen, ended the call, and
tossed the phone to the ground. His hold was as strong
as Eli's—maybe stronger. Trying to get out of it was
futile.

"Who'd you call?" he asked.

I heard his question, but I was too busy watching the
girl pull the crystal wand out of her shoulder as easily as
one might pull a pin from their hair to answer. How did

she do that? Blood dripped everywhere—I must have hit an artery. But the wound was knitting together, healing in front of my eyes.

"That's not possible." I shook my head, trying to make sense of what I'd seen. But there was no way to make sense of it.

Was I hallucinating again?

Maybe. But her blood was still on the floor. I'd felt the crystal wand break through her skin. Now she was standing up, unharmed. And the man was acting like this was totally normal.

This was real. I didn't know *how* it was real, but it was. I knew it in my gut.

Which meant everything that had happened in the alley was real, too.

"Was there someone here earlier?" the man holding me asked. "The older man from the alley?"

"Are you working with him?" I tried to twist around to look at him, but it was hopeless, so I directed the question toward the girl instead. "Did he take my mom?"

"He took your mom?" Her eyebrows shot up in surprise.

The man spun me around so I was facing him. He stared down at me with his deep brown eyes and gripped my shoulders, holding me in place. "We're *hunting* that man, not working with him," he said. "We followed his trail here. Do you know why he wanted your mom?"

"No," I said. "But I called the cops. They'll be here soon. They'll figure out what happened to her."

They had to.

"We can't be here when the cops arrive." The girl walked to the balcony and glanced out the open door. "We need to get out of here."

"Fine." The man followed her, dragging me along. "But she comes with us."

"What?" the girl and I said at the same time. She glared at me, as if wondering how I dared say the same thing as her, and looked to him for an answer.

"She might be able to help us figure out what the greater demon wants with her mom," he said.

"Demon?" I sputtered and tried to pull away, but he held me locked in place. "Are you saying that a *demon* took my mom?"

"Yes." He held his gaze with mine, like he was daring me to contradict him.

"That's ridiculous," I said. "Demons don't exist."

"Wrong," he said. "Or have you already forgotten how I saved you from one and disintegrated him back in the alley?"

My eyes widened. It *had* been real.

How would he have known what had happened

otherwise?

"We don't have time for this." The girl glanced out the balcony, looking worried. "We need to leave. Now."

"Who *are* you guys?" I looked back and forth between them with a mix of wonder and terror. "You move so fast, you turned that man into ash, and you *healed* in front of my eyes. None of that should be possible."

"We're the ones who can help you find your mom." The man towered over me, his grip around my arm tightening. "The police can't help you. We can. But if you want our help, you need to come with us." He watched me so intensely—so *desperately*—that I knew he was telling the truth.

I looked past him to the kitchen table, where the Chariot tarot card was still face up in the same spot it had been during my final conversation with my mom. What had she told me regarding the card?

She'd told me to be prepared for upcoming changes, and to be receptive of the new people who came into my life because of those changes.

She'd also told me to remember that I was the Charioteer of my own life, and not to let anyone take that power from me.

"Well?" The girl threw her hands up in the air, scowling at me. "Are you coming or not?"

Logic said I should wait for the cops to arrive—not run off with two leather-clad intruders who may or may not have superpowers. Who knew where they'd take me? Maybe this was all an elaborate plot so they could abduct me, too.

But I'd seen how strong they were—I could feel it in the man's grip. If they'd wanted to take me, I would have been halfway back to their lair by now.

Instead, they were giving me a choice.

Most importantly, the man seemed to truly believe that they were the only ones who could help me find my mom.

"If I go with you, will you answer all my questions?" I asked, matching his steely gaze with one of my own.

"We can't—" the girl started.

"As long as you answer ours in return, then once we're back to the compound, yes, we'll answer your questions," he cut his companion off, glaring at her as if telling her to shut up with his mind.

Maybe he *had* told her to shut up with his mind. After all, they did have superpowers.

Add telepathy to my growing list of questions I had for them.

"All right." The decision felt *right* once the words were out of my mouth. "Let's go."

17

RAVEN

HE THREW me over his back, ran to the balcony, and jumped over the ledge.

I screamed and squeezed my eyes shut, preparing for the worst. But he landed as lightly as a feather, as if he'd jumped one step down instead of one *story* down.

He released me from his back, and my feet hit the pavement, my body shaking. Both he and the girl hopped onto their motorcycles like they were performing some sort of choreographed dance.

He revved the engine and looked at me. "Are you coming or what?" he asked.

"I need my stuff." I glanced back up at the open doors of the balcony. "My phone, my wallet... they're inside the apartment."

"We don't have time for this." The girl glared at me. "I

85

hear the sirens in the distance. Get on Noah's bike, or we're leaving without you."

My mysterious savior had a name—Noah.

I liked it. It fit him well.

"The Montgomery pack will take care of you," Noah said confidently. "But Sage is right. We need to leave —now."

I bit my lip and wrapped my arms around myself, feeling naked without my stuff. Going anywhere without my phone, ID, and credit cards was downright stupid. *Especially* given that I knew nothing about these people, or the Montgomery pack they'd mentioned.

But if Noah and Sage left me here, I'd lose this chance of finding my mom.

I had to suck it up and trust them.

So I hopped on the back of his bike and wrapped my arms around his waist, holding on for dear life. The moment I was on, he pulled out of the drive. The girl— Sage—followed close behind.

My hair whipped behind us as we sped down the main street. Two police cars passed on the opposite side of the road, speeding toward the apartment.

They must have been the ones dispatched by 911.

Deep down, my heart told me that going with Noah and Sage was the right decision. They had supernatural abilities, and whoever had taken my mom—the *demon*, they'd said—clearly had them too.

I was entering completely uncharted territory.

But as the sound of sirens disappeared into the distance, I couldn't help wondering if I'd just made a terrible mistake.

18

RAVEN

It didn't strike me until we hit the freeway that I had no idea where we were heading. They'd mentioned a compound, but that was all I knew. So I held on tight for the entire forty minute ride that eventually took us all the way up into the Hollywood Hills.

The winding roads, full trees, and open land in the Hills seemed like a completely different world than Venice Beach. Noah drove and drove up the hills until pulling up to a house all the way at the top.

Well, "house," was an understatement. Like they'd said, it was a sprawling compound.

Sage stopped outside the thick wooden gate, and Noah followed her lead. She shook out her hair, running her fingers through it to brush out any knots.

I tried to do the same to my hair, but it was a hopeless mess.

"Welcome to the Montgomery compound," she said to me, her tone grim. Without waiting for a response, she turned to Noah and asked, "What are you planning on telling the pack? They'll freak out when they realize you've brought a human here."

"We couldn't just leave her back there," Noah said. "Not after everything she saw."

"She would have figured out a way to rationalize it," she said. "They all do."

"My name's Raven," I cut in, and Sage whipped her head to look at me, as if surprised I had the audacity to speak to her at all. "In case you were wondering."

"I'm Noah," Noah said. "And that's—"

"Sage," I interrupted. "I got that part."

She nodded at me briefly before flicking her gaze back to Noah. "You still haven't answered my question," she said. "What's the plan?"

"I'm not sure yet," he said. "I figured we'd bring her back to the pool house, ask her some questions to try to figure out what that demon wanted with her mom, and work it out from there."

My throat tightened at the mention of my mom, and I swallowed, blinking away tears.

They'd help me find her. We *had* to find her.

"They'll smell her the moment she steps foot on the property." Sage sighed, removed a black ring from her finger, and held it out to me. "Here," she said. "Put this on."

"Why?" I asked.

"It's for your protection," she said. "Noah will explain once you're inside."

I hated trusting people blindly. But I'd already come this far. And what harm could come from putting on a ring?

I took it from her and slid it onto my finger.

Noah's eyes didn't leave my hand until the ring was secure. "Good," he said, turning back to Sage. "What'll you be doing while I'm with her in the pool house?"

"I'll be in the main house, stopping anyone from wandering into the pool house before we figure out a way to break it to them that not only are you letting a human in on our secrets, but that you're stashing her away on Montgomery pack property."

19

RAVEN

SAGE PARKED her bike in the massive garage—it looked huge enough to fit ten cars. Noah continued around the garage and toward the pool, stopping at a small house off to the side.

We hopped off the bike, and as he propped it against the wall I turned around, taking in the view. From the top of the hill, I could see the entire city skyline, vibrant and lit up with life.

"It's something, isn't it?" Noah said from behind me.

"Yeah." I wrapped my arms around myself and took a deep breath of the cool, crisp air, glad to have one minute of calm in this crazy, hectic night. "It's beautiful."

"I guess." He shrugged. "I never knew so many people could fit into one place."

"You're not from here?" I asked.

"No." His eyes darkened, and he looked away from the view, as if regretting he'd said anything at all. "Come on. Let's get you inside before anyone spots you."

I followed him into the pool house, noticing that he wore a black ring that matched the one Sage had given me. Strange.

Were they *together*? Was that why they wore matching rings?

But his ring was on his right hand—he wore nothing on his left. Which meant he was single.

I shook the thought from my head, embarrassed to be wondering if Noah was single at a time like this.

Maybe it was my mind's way of coping with all the crazy stuff that had been thrown at me in one night.

He took off his jacket, flung it on the closest chair, and walked to the mini-fridge to pull out a beer. He opened it and took a sip. Then turned to me, as if just remembering I was standing there. "Want one?" he asked, holding his beer up to show what he meant.

"Just water's fine." I still felt a bit dizzy from the drinks I'd had earlier, and I wanted a clear head when he answered my growing list of questions.

I shoved my hands into my back pockets and looked around as he grabbed my drink. The inside of the pool house was compact, with a living area, bathroom, bedroom, and miniature kitchen. The decorations were sparse—I didn't see any photos or anything other than bland, generic artwork.

"Do you live here?" I asked.

"For now." He handed me a glass of water—he'd put a lot of ice in it, just how I liked it.

My fingers brushed his as I took it from him, and warmth rushed through my body at his touch. I broke contact quickly, glancing away. He might be hot—okay, he was *definitely* hot—but I wasn't going to let his rugged, movie star looks distract me from getting to the bottom of what had happened tonight.

I downed the water in nearly one gulp. Apparently I was thirstier than I'd realized. Once done, I placed the glass on the end table, ready to get down to business.

"Where's my mom?" I asked. "You said you could find her. So where is she?"

"I don't know where she is." He leaned against the counter and took another sip of his beer. He was so casual about it, as if his words didn't make it feel like the entire world was crumbling around me.

"What?" I crossed my arms, glaring at him. "You told me you could find her."

"I told you I was your best chance at finding her," he said. "I never said I knew where she was."

"But you know who took her?"

"She was taken by a demon," he said. "And not just

any demon—a *greater* demon. The same one who tried to take you in that alley."

"A demon," I repeated, still trying to get it through my mind. "Like an actual, real demon? With horns? From Hell?"

"Yep. Except for the horns part. Demons don't have horns."

"Okay." I took a deep breath and ran my fingers through my hair. This was crazy—I was still barely making sense of it—but I had to try. For my mom's sake. "What does a demon want with my mom?"

"That's what I was hoping you could help me figure out." He walked over to the armchair and sat down, reclining his feet on the coffee table like this was a normal conversation to have over a beer.

I didn't know if he expected me to join him, but I remained standing. There was no way I could relax when my mom's life was at risk.

"How can I help you figure that out?" I raised my voice, my frustration growing and growing with each passing second. "I don't know anything about demons— I didn't even think they *existed* until today."

"You didn't know they existed until they tried to take you from that restaurant," he said. "They didn't just want your mom—they wanted you, too. You really don't know why?"

"No!" I was full out yelling now, my frustration and anger feeling like it was about to erupt out of my skin.

"Keep your voice down." He narrowed his eyes at me. "You don't want the others to hear."

"The pool house is *across the property* from the main house!" I pointed to where the main house was— farther away than anyone could possibly hear, especially through closed doors. "How could they hear me? Or here's a better question—how did Sage heal so quickly back in my room? How did the two of you jump off my second floor balcony without a scratch on you? How did you stab that guy in the alley and *turn him into dust*? How did you even know to be in that alley at the exact right time to save my life, *and* in my apartment after my mom had been taken?" I dropped my arm back to my side, needing to take a breath.

"That's a lot of questions." He chuckled, still casually sipping on his beer like he was watching a sports game with his friends. "I already told you the answer to the last one. Sage and I knew to be in that alley and at your apartment because we're hunting demons."

"So you're demon hunters?" I asked. "That's why you have all those… powers?"

It sounded ridiculous, but I knew what I saw.

"I'm currently hunting for demons, and Sage is

helping me out," he said. "But the details of that situation aren't relevant right now."

"What?" I glared at him. I hated when anyone talked down to me, even if that person *had* saved my life twice in one night. "Why aren't they *relevant?*"

"Because if you want to find your mom, then I need to do the asking and you need to do the answering."

"You promised to answer my questions if I came with you." I laid my hands flat on the back of the sofa, staring down at him.

"I said I'd answer your questions if you answered mine first." He smirked and raised an eyebrow, making me want to wipe the arrogance right off his face. "Do you want to find your mom or not?"

"Of course I want to find her."

"That's what I thought." He motioned to the couch next to him. "So calm down, stop yelling, and take a seat. It's my turn to do the asking."

20

RAVEN

I sat down on the couch and crossed my arms, waiting for him to begin.

"That's better," he said.

I wanted to say something that would erase the gloating look off his face. But he was going to help me find my mom, so I held my tongue and said nothing.

"You ready?" he asked.

"Do you think I'm sitting here for the fun of it?"

"You're not?" He raised his beer in a toast. "You had me fooled."

I uncrossed my arms and slammed my hands down next to me. "Are you serious about finding my mom or not?" I asked.

"I am," he said.

"Why?" I leaned forward, leveling my gaze with his. "You don't know her. Who is she to you?"

"Like I said, I'm hunting demons," he said. "The demons are hunting something of their own, but I'm not sure what that something is. The demons hunted both you and your mom, so apparently you're connected to that something. I want to figure out why the demons hunted you—specifically, *what* they're after that the two of you have—so I can use it as bait to make my hunts go faster."

"All right." I nodded, satisfied with that response. "What do you need to know?"

"You said you've never seen a demon before—that you didn't know they existed before today," he said. "But do you—or your mom—have any connections to the supernatural world?"

"What do you mean by the 'supernatural world?'" I asked. "Do you come from another *planet*? Are you aliens? Is that why you and Sage have all those powers?"

I'd always believed in aliens—it seemed incredibly improbable that Earth was the only planet in the universe with life—so this explanation was more believable than anything else that had crossed my mind so far.

He looked at me like I'd lost my mind and said nothing, as if waiting for me to take it back. "You're serious, aren't you?" he finally asked.

I narrowed my eyes at him, not liking his tone. "It's as good of an explanation as any," I said.

"We're not aliens," he said. "The supernatural world is the world of supernaturals that lives alongside the human world in secret. Demons, angels, vampires, shifters, witches... *that's* the supernatural world."

"And hunters?" I asked. "Like you and Sage?"

He said nothing for a few moments, just staring at me with those super intense brooding eyes of his.

"I ask." He pointed at himself, then turned his finger around to point at me. "You answer. That was our deal."

I pressed my lips together—I hadn't *meant* to turn the table around on him again. It had just happened.

But while stopping myself from asking questions was difficult, I needed to try. For my mom's sake.

So I said nothing, instead just sitting there and waiting for him to continue.

"Do you and your mom have any connections to our world?" he repeated.

I was about to say no, but I stopped myself. Because to help Noah find my mom, I needed to be honest. And after everything I'd witnessed tonight, I could no longer deny what my mom had been telling me about our heritage for my entire life.

"My mom's a witch." I glanced down at my hands, my cheeks flushing with embarrassment. This was the first time I'd ever said it and wondered if it might be the truth. "She says I am too. We're descended from a long line of witches that goes back to the witch trials in Europe. One of our ancestors was killed for witchcraft in Ireland—it was a big reason why our family came over to the States."

Noah's brow creased, and he looked at me in disbelief—like he was waiting for me to say I was kidding.

"Why are you looking at me like that?" I asked. "My mom and I being witches is hardly the strangest thing that's happened tonight."

"You're not a witch," he said simply. "Neither is your mom."

"You don't know that." I didn't know why I was going on the defensive—I'd never believed that my mom was a witch, either—but it was different when this guy who didn't know me was acting like he knew more about my family than I did.

"Yes, I do," he said. "If you were a witch, I'd smell it. You're a human. And your apartment smelled nothing like witch. Meaning your mom is human, too."

"So you can *smell* the difference between humans and witches?" I asked.

"I can," he said.

"Is this another hunter ability?"

"Yes," he said, shocking me by actually answering one of my questions.

"What do witches smell like?" I asked. "And what do humans smell like?"

"Witches smell sweet, like flowers," he said. "Or syrup, depending on what type of witch they are. Humans smell like meat." Hunger shined in his gaze, and I wrapped my arms around myself, suddenly uncomfortable.

What kind of hunter was he that he was looking at me like that?

Maybe my instinct to run from him in that alley was correct.

"So I smell like food to you?" I asked.

"We're getting off track again." He sipped his beer, and the hunger in his eyes vanished, replaced by the determination from earlier. "Other than your mom believing you're from a line of witches, you have no connection to the supernatural world, right?"

"Not that I know of," I said.

"All right," he said. "So, tell me about your day today. Start from the beginning, and don't leave out any details."

"Why?" I asked.

"Can't get rid of that curiosity, can you?" He sighed,

continuing before I could answer. "Something about you and your mom sparked the demons' interest in you. If you tell me the details of your day, maybe I can figure out what that something was."

"Okay," I said, and I launched into the details of my day, starting from when I'd woken up in the morning.

He stopped me after the tarot reading my mom had given me in the apartment.

"So both you and your mom are able to read the cards?" he asked.

"It's basic psychology," I said. "Ask a person the right questions, and it's easy to relate the cards to their life."

"But you and your mom drew the same cards in a reading about yourself," he said. "That sounds like more than psychology."

"Yeah," I agreed. "It *was* weird. Especially since the cards were right."

"Hm." He stared off at the wall, then returned his focus to me. "What happened next?"

"My friends and I went to the Santa Monica Pier," I said. "Once we got there, we asked this guy to take a picture of us, but he was a real jerk and said no. So we found someone else to take the picture instead."

I couldn't help myself from tossing that in there. I tilted my head and looked at him with complete innocence as I waited for his response.

"Sage and I were on a hunt," he said. "We didn't have time to waste taking pictures for a group of college girls."

"I know," I said. "I get it now."

From there, I told him about the rest of the night, ending at when I'd ran back into the restaurant and told my friends about what had happened.

"After that, you went straight back to your house?" he asked.

"Yeah," I said. "They took me home."

"Did anything happen on the way from the restaurant back to the house?"

"No," I started, but then I stopped. "Actually, that's not true. There was this psychic who'd tried to get me to come into her booth for a free palm reading when we were on our way to dinner. She knew my name—I figured I'd helped her at the store at some point. But when we were heading back, she ran up to me and grabbed me. She said something about having all the answers and that she'll be waiting for me to return so she can answer my questions. The whole thing was pretty creepy, especially since she was blind. I have no idea how she knew I was walking by."

Noah sat straighter as I finished up, looking like he was on to something. "This blind psychic," he said. "Did you catch her name?"

"Yes," I said. "Rosella."

He stood up, crossed the room, and grabbed his jacket. "Come on," he said. "We're leaving."

"What?" I stood too, my heart leaping at the possibility that Noah might know something that could help him find my mom. "Where are we going?"

"We're going to Rosella," he said as he put on his jacket. "You said she had a booth at the Santa Monica Pier?"

"You really think some teenage girl who works at the fair is connected to all of this?" I asked.

"Rosella isn't just some teenage girl who works at the fair," he said. "She's a centuries' old vampire with the ability to see the future."

"A *vampire?*" I repeated. "Are you serious?"

At the same time, I couldn't help remembering how dead her skin had felt when she'd touched me. Like she wasn't alive. Wasn't *human*.

"No," he said. "I'm making it up for my own amusement."

"You're being sarcastic," I said.

"Of course I am." He swung his keys around his finger and headed for the door. "And once the others realize you're here, they're going to have questions. So if you want to get to Rosella as soon as possible, we need to leave. Now."

That was all I needed to convince me to hop back behind him on the bike and hold on tight for the return drive to the Pier.

21

RAVEN

WE ARRIVED at the Pier after midnight.

The amusement park section was dark, since it had closed hours ago. But the Pier itself was open for all hours, so a few of the shops and restaurants remained open.

Rosella's was among those few.

We stepped through the small door and found her sitting at a table with a middle-aged woman, giving her a palm reading. "Your lifeline is long," she said as she ran a finger over the woman's palm. "You're going to live to a nice, old age until eventually passing in your sleep. But don't let this knowledge stop you from living in the moment or asking for forgiveness from past mistakes. People are more forgiving than you realize. And above all else, always remember to appreciate life and the time spent with those you love."

"Thank you." The lady smiled. "I'll remember that." She thanked Rosella again, paid, and headed out.

"I've been expecting you." Rosella didn't turn to look at Noah and me as she spoke. "Please, sit." She stood up, closed the door, and switched the sign in the window from open to closed.

Noah and I took a seat on the deep red sofa that looked like something from an antique shop. He sat as far away from me as possible.

Did I smell bad or something? I'd showered that morning, but a *lot* had happened since then. I hadn't bothered looking in a mirror since the bathroom at the restaurant, but I was surely looking—and smelling—far from my best.

"That poor lady," Rosella said as she situated herself in the antique chair across from us. "She's going to be killed by a drunk driver eight months from now."

"What?" I widened my eyes, shocked. "Why didn't you say so? You could have stopped it from happening."

"Just because one can see the future doesn't mean they should meddle with it," she said. "The future is like a finely woven tapestry. Unravel one string, and the rest come undone as well. I learned that lesson the hard way in my first decade as a seer. However, what I said to her will help her mend relationships she thought were permanently broken, and live these final few months to the fullest. It won't save her life, but it *will* make a positive difference in the months she has left to live."

I nodded, although I was unsure about how I felt about all of that.

"Anyway, we're not here to talk about her—we're here to talk about you." Rosella faced me, staring blankly with her milky eyes.

I hadn't taken a good look at her before. Now, I was surprised by how young and frail she was. She appeared to be fourteen or fifteen, tops.

It was hard to believe she was a real, live *vampire*.

I shifted in my seat, suddenly uncomfortable. Because vampires drank blood to survive—*human* blood. She'd closed down shop and no one knew I was here.

My instinct told me to flee.

On the other hand, Noah had kept me safe from the demons, so I trusted he would keep me safe from a vampire, too. But she was still the predator, and I, the prey. It was definitely enough to make me antsy.

"You don't need to be so nervous," Rosella said. "I survive solely off of animal blood. I haven't tasted human blood since the completion of my change into a vampire centuries ago."

I glanced at Noah to verify if she was telling the truth.

"Rosella's allegiance is to the kingdom of the Haven," he said. "Haven vampires drink only animal blood. You're safe with her. I wouldn't have brought you here if you weren't." His gaze intensified, as if it angered him to think I suspected him of bringing me somewhere dangerous.

"Okay." I relaxed and turned back to Rosella, eager to get to the point. "I need to know where my mom is."

I figured there was no need to tell her that my mom was taken by a demon. Since she was a seer, she should already know why I was here.

"Your mother has been taken by the greater demon Azazel," she said. "I believe you met him earlier tonight in the alley behind the Mexican restaurant on this Pier."

"The man in the leather jacket," I realized. "The one who took my mom's necklace." I reached for where the crystal had been on my skin, although of course there was nothing there.

"Yes," she said. "That was Azazel."

"My mom's okay, right?" I asked the question that had been torturing me since discovering she'd been taken. "She's still alive?"

"She's alive," Rosella confirmed.

I noticed she didn't verify she was okay, but just

knowing she was alive made me breathe slightly easier. "Why take her?" I asked. "What does this Azazel want with my mom?"

"You're asking the wrong questions," the seer said simply.

"Seriously?" I threw my hands down on the couch. Everything inside me was wound up tight, and I felt close to the edge of shattering. "My mom's been taken by a *demon*. I just want to know how to get her back."

"That's the question I was waiting for." Rosella sat straighter and smiled in approval. "Because to get your mom back, you must go to the island of Avalon."

22

RAVEN

"THAT'S where my mom's been taken?" I asked. "Avalon?"

"No," Rosella said. "Avalon is where you must go if you want to find your mom."

"But where *is* she?" I fiddled with my hands—I was getting beyond impatient with her roundabout answers.

"I'm afraid I do not know," Rosella said. "There's a barrier keeping me from seeing her location. But if you want to save her, you need to get to Avalon. That, I can say for sure."

"All right." I dropped my hands to my sides and got ahold of myself, since this was the best start I had right now. "So where's Avalon?"

"It's an island in the Atlantic Ocean," she said. "Only the members of the Earth Angel's army—or those who have chosen to go through the trials to join the Earth Angel's army—can get there."

"What's an Earth Angel?" I asked.

"She's a person," Noah said. "Her name is Annika. She was a Nephilim until the angels in Heaven turned her into a full angel. But since she was born on Earth and not in Heaven, she's the only angel who can walk the Earth."

"And she has an army?" I asked.

"Yes." He didn't elaborate further.

"Why?" If he thought I was going to leave it at that, he still hadn't realized who he was dealing with. "Who's she fighting?"

"The demons," he said. "Earlier this year, hundreds of demons were released from Hell and onto Earth. Now, supernaturals everywhere are going to Avalon to join the Earth Angel's army to stop the demons from reaching their ultimate goal."

"Which is...?"

"To kill all supernaturals, rule over Earth, and take humans as their slaves."

"Whoa." I sat back in shock. "Are you serious?"

But as I asked, I knew he was. Because this had to be the darkness my mom had felt.

She'd told me all of this herself earlier. She'd *been*

saying stuff like this for weeks. Why hadn't I believed her?

And if she wasn't a witch, how was she able to sense that all of this was happening?

"He is," Rosella confirmed. "The situation is dire, but as long as the Earth Angel's army is there to fight the demons, hope isn't lost."

"And you want me to go to Avalon." I swallowed, still confused. "Even though only supernaturals can get there?"

"Only members of the Earth Angel's army and those who have chosen to go through the trials to join the Earth Angel's army can get to Avalon," Rosella repeated what she'd said before. "Humans can choose to join the trials. If they pass, they'll be turned into Nephilim."

"Hold up." I held a hand up, unsure if I understood this properly. "To save my mom, I need to go to Avalon. But only members of the Earth Angel's army or those who are going through the trials to join the Earth Angel's army can get there. So you're saying that to save my mom... I need to go through these trials and join her army?"

"That seems like the most logical solution." Rosella gave me a closed lipped smile. "Does it not?"

"But I just want to find my mom," I said. "I don't want to join an army."

"To find your mom, you must go to Avalon," Rosella repeated.

"I know that." I ran my hands through my hair, frustration erupting through my veins. "But isn't there another way to get there? One that doesn't involve going through trials in an attempt to become a… what did you call it again?"

"A Nephilim," Noah jumped in.

"I don't even know what a Nephilim is!" I was yelling now, and I didn't care. Because there *had* to be an easier way to save my mom.

This was way more complicated than anything I'd thought I was signing up for.

"Nephilim are humans with angel blood in their veins," Rosella said. "The angel blood gives them supernatural abilities, like strength, speed, and more. They're perfectly designed to hunt and kill demons. Nephilim are the most valued members of the army, because while any supernatural can kill regular demons as long as they're wielding a heavenly weapon, only Nephilim can kill greater demons."

"Is that what you are?" I asked Noah. "A Nephilim?"

"No." He turned away from me, not meeting my eyes.

He was keeping something from me, and I was going to find out what it was. But for now, I needed to know more about Avalon and the Nephilim.

"So to save my mom, I have to go to Avalon and become one of these Nephilim." The more I said it, the more I realized I was accepting it.

I would do *anything* to save her—even this.

"Yes," Rosella said. "Your path is your choice—it's *always* your choice—but that is the path that leads to the highest likelihood of saving your mom."

"Fine." I straightened. "I'll do it. How do I get to Avalon?"

"Noah can lead the way," Rosella said with a knowing smile. "It just so happens that he's heading to Avalon as well."

"Great." I turned to Noah, eager to get started. "When do we leave?"

"We don't," he said simply. "At least, not anytime soon."

23

RAVEN

"WHAT?" I slammed a hand against the couch. "I thought you were going there too."

"I am," he said. "But there's a bit of a complication."

"Go on." I sat back and crossed my arms, waiting for him to continue.

"Before going to Avalon, I need to complete a task given to me by the Earth Angel," he said. "I need to kill ten demons and bring a tooth from each of them to her as evidence. Only then will I be allowed on the island. I've killed six so far, so I've got four more to go."

"That's why you're hunting demons," I realized. "For admittance to Avalon."

He nodded, which I assumed meant I was correct.

"Does everyone have to complete a task to get onto Avalon?" I asked.

If they did, that meant one more step I'd have to take to save my mom.

"Not everyone," he said, although he left it at that.

"All right," I said. "Then can someone else take me to Avalon?"

"No," Rosella cut in. "You must go with Noah."

"Why?" Noah and I asked at the same time.

I looked over at him, and he glared at me before looking away.

What was his problem? It was like he was angry at me for just *thinking* the same thing as him.

"Raven will join you on the remainder of your hunt," Rosella said. "She'll need the experience if she hopes to pass the Angel Trials."

Shivers raced down my spine at the sound of that. "What happens if I don't pass the Angel Trials?" I asked.

"The details will be explained by members of the Earth Angel's army before you enter Avalon," she said. "That's when you'll decide if you want to take part in the trials or not. You're only allowed onto Avalon if you agree to participate."

"Then the details don't matter," I said. "Because I'm getting to Avalon, which means I'm participating in those trials."

"Stupid," Noah muttered from next to me.

"Really?" I whipped my head to the side and glared at

him. "Since when was it *stupid* to do everything I can to save someone I love?"

"You're jumping in blind." He rested his elbows on his knees, his eyes intense as he stared me down. "It's stupid. Not that it matters, because you're not coming with me on my hunt."

"Why not?" I asked. "Didn't you hear what Rosella said? Going with you will give me the best chance to pass the Angel Trials."

"And babysitting you on my hunt will slow me down," he said. "You're not coming."

We held each other's gazes, neither of us backing down. I felt like I was in some kind of dominance staring contest—like if I broke eye contact with him, I'd lose.

"If she doesn't go with you, she won't pass the Angel Trials," Rosella finally said.

"Why should I care?" Noah broke his gaze with mine to focus on Rosella. "She's just some human I saved from a demon. She's not my problem."

I gasped, his words stinging like a knife to the chest. After everything that had happened tonight, I'd thought Noah was on my side. I'd thought there was some kind of connection between us. I'd *trusted* him. Not just with my life, but with my mom's, too.

I felt beyond stupid for that now.

"If I'm 'not your problem,' why didn't you leave me back at my apartment?" I asked. "That's what Sage wanted to do, right?"

"I couldn't just leave you there," he said. "Not when you might have been able to help me figure out what the demons are hunting."

"I might still be able to help you figure out what they're hunting." My eyes welled with tears as I looked at him, begging him to reconsider. I hated that it was coming to begging, but if Rosella was right, Noah was my best shot at getting to my mom. "Just give me a chance. Please."

He watched me closely, looking like he was thinking about it.

Then he turned back to Rosella.

"You think I should take her with me?" he asked her.

"I can't force you to do anything you don't want to do," she said. "But I think I've made it clear that I think you should bring Raven on your journey."

"Fine." Noah turned back to me, not looking too happy about it. "You can come."

"Really?" I held my breath, afraid he was about to take it back.

"Really," he said. "Mainly because the seer says so, but also because I wouldn't have this opportunity to get to

Avalon if someone hadn't given *me* a chance. So I guess I'll give you one. But Raven?"

"Yeah?" My stomach dropped, and I braced myself for whatever he was about to say next.

"Don't make me regret this."

24

RAVEN

When we returned to the compound, a group of about ten people stood at the gate, blocking our entrance.

Noah placed his feet down on the sides of the bike and stared at them. I kept my arms tightly around his waist. I didn't have a good feeling about this, but I was curious, so I peered around him to observe the others.

Sage stood in the middle of the group. Next to her was the tallest man of them all, his muscles so large that he looked like he could rip a person apart with his bare hands. He was like a tanner twin of the Rock.

The others were still intimidating, but less so. Equal amount males and females, they were all dressed in leather and expensive-looking denim, just like Noah and Sage. Most of them had their arms crossed or on their

121

hips, staring us down like we were kids who'd gotten home after curfew.

I supposed this was the "pack" that Noah and Sage had mentioned earlier—the group they were trying to keep me from meeting until the time was right.

Noah zeroed in on Sage. "You told them." He said it as a statement, not a question.

"Flint knew something was up." She motioned to the tall body builder next to her—I assumed he was Flint. "He noticed my ring was gone, and he could smell Raven on me. Then he came outside and smelled her around the gate. He figured out what we did."

Flint cracked his knuckles and stared at me like I was a piece of meat. "You know the rules," he said, turning his gaze to Noah. "No one comes back to the compound without my permission. Especially not a human."

I tightened my grip around Noah's waist, not daring to speak. I hated backing down in front of anyone, but Flint was the most intimidating person I'd ever seen. I had a feeling that one wrong move would have him flattening me to the pavement.

"I'm sorry." Noah lowered his eyes—it was like he purposefully wasn't meeting Flint's gaze. "The demons targeted Raven and her mom. They took her mom, but I was able to get Raven to safety. I don't know why those demons targeted them, but they *must* have a reason.

Finding out that reason will benefit my mission—a mission that helps us *all*. So I had to bring her with me to figure out why she was a target."

"Sage already told us everything—don't repeat it all and bore me to death." Flint's teeth glinted in the moonlight as he spoke.

I glared at Sage. Wasn't she supposed to have been on our side?

She lowered her eyes, unwilling to even look at me.

Apparently, Flint was the king of this compound, and whatever he said or did was law.

"Where did you go with the human?" Flint asked Noah. "And why did you bring her back here?"

"We went to see Rosella." Noah spoke calmly and steadily, still not looking straight at Flint.

Flint tilted his head, looking doubtful. "The seer of the Haven?" he asked.

"Yes," Noah said.

"But she lives at the Haven." Flint stepped forward and pounded his fist into his palm, the loud smack cracking through the air. "In *India*."

Noah didn't flinch. "Tonight, she was at the Santa Monica Pier," he said. "She sought out Raven specifically. When I was briefing Raven, she told me about a run-in she had earlier with Rosella. We had to go to the seer at once."

"And what did the seer say?" Flint asked.

"Why don't we go inside?" Noah said. "I'll fill you in there."

"Fine." Flint shot me one more glare. "But she's only allowed in temporarily. And sweetheart?" he asked, turning his focus to me.

I swallowed, nervous about where he was going with this. "Yes?" I asked, since from the way he was leering at me, I could tell he wanted a response.

"While you're in the compound, you keep that ring on." He smiled, showing off his perfect teeth. "I'm not responsible for anything that might happen to you if you don't."

25

RAVEN

THE MAIN HOUSE WAS GINORMOUS—THE compound clearly had enough bedrooms for all ten of them, plus some extra rooms to spare. We settled in the living room area. The entire house was earthy and fresh, with hardwood floors, leather furniture, and various animal heads mounted on the walls. I felt like I was inside a ski lodge instead of a mansion on top of the Hollywood Hills.

Noah sat on a loveseat, and I took the spot next to him. Sage grabbed the chair on his other side. Flint, of course, sat smack in the center of the main sofa. The rest of them filled in the spots that were left.

There was a group of about three of them, two males and a female, who stayed as far from me as possible.

They barely even looked at me. If I didn't know better, I'd think they were scared of me.

Which was ridiculous. I'd seen what Noah and Sage could do. If their friends could do even half the things they could, they had no reason to be scared of *me*.

Once we were situated, Noah filled them in on what we'd learned during our visit with Rosella.

"Are you crazy?" Sage said once he'd finished. "Raven's a human. She can't come with us on our hunts."

"I can, and I will." I tried to stay as calm as possible, not in the mood to fight over this again. "I'll try my best not to slow him down. I promise. I want to get to Avalon just as badly as Noah does."

"First of all, you have no idea how badly Noah wants to get to Avalon, because you have no idea why he wants to go at all," she said. "Secondly, the problem isn't that you're going to slow us down. It's that you're going to get yourself killed."

"I was there today when you hunted that demon, and I'm still here." I straightened, irritated that she thought so little of me. "I might not be strong like you all, but I'm smart and resilient. I can hold my own."

"Your escape tonight was luck," Sage muttered. "If we'd gotten there a minute later, you would have been handed off to that greater demon and teleported who knows where. I don't care how smart you might be—

you're no match for a greater demon. If we hadn't saved you, you'd be in the same spot as your mother."

The mention of my mom was like a knife in the heart, and I jolted back at the harshness of her words. Especially because what she'd said was true.

"That's enough." Noah narrowed his eyes at Sage. "Rosella recommended that I bring Raven with me on my hunt, so she's coming with me. End of discussion."

I nodded at him in thanks, surprised that he'd stood up for me after how adamant he'd been at first about *not* wanting me to come with him.

He turned his gaze away from mine, not acknowledging my thanks in the slightest.

"Well, if you're both going, then I guess I'm going, too," Sage said with a sigh.

"Are you sure that's a good idea?" Flint stared her down—he clearly didn't want her to go. "From what I've heard about this human, she sounds like she attracts trouble. We don't need to be bringing any trouble down on our pack."

There was that word again—*pack*.

I wanted to ask why they kept calling themselves that, but there was so much animosity in the room that I kept my mouth shut. For now. I'd definitely be asking Noah about it the next time we were alone.

There was a *lot* I still needed to ask him the next time we were alone.

"We don't hunt alone." Sage held Flint's gaze. "You know that."

"Noah won't be alone, because I'll be there with him," I said to Sage. I hated how she was acting like I was no one.

Compared to their superpowers, I probably *was* no one, but still. I didn't like being ignored.

"Humans don't count," she said. "If anything, the fact that Noah will be worrying about keeping you safe *while* hunting demons is more of a reason for me to come along as backup."

"Sage." Flint's eyes were hard as he looked at her—as if she were in trouble. Everyone quieted the moment he spoke. "Perhaps the time has come for you to leave Noah to his mission and stay home."

"No way." She crossed her arms, clearly not about to back down. "I started this mission with Noah, so I'm going to end it with him, too."

"You should remain home with the pack," he said. "Noah's mission isn't your problem."

"His mission *is* my problem!" she said. "It's *all* of our problems. You all know as well as I do that even though the demons are laying low for now, they eventually want to kill all supernaturals. We can't keep sitting up here in our compound doing nothing."

"What exactly do you plan on doing?" Flint asked. "Going with Noah to Avalon and joining the Earth Angel's army as well?"

"Maybe." Sage jutted her chin out. "I don't want to— obviously I'd prefer to stay home—but I also want to make sure we *have* a home at all. If that means going to Avalon and joining the army, then so be it."

Noah bristled, looking surprised by Sage's statement. The two of them met eyes and stared at each other for a few seconds. Again, it was like they were having a conversation without speaking.

Jealously surged through my veins. What was going on between Noah and Sage?

It was stupid of me to care. Not only did Noah clearly not see me that way, but Sage was strong, beautiful, and fierce. If there was something between them, I never stood a chance.

I also shouldn't be thinking about my attraction to Noah when there was so much more at stake. So I shook the thought out of my head, forcing myself to pay attention to the conversation at hand.

"The Montgomery pack will *not* sit by and do nothing," Flint said. "You, my sister, should know me well enough to know that."

I sat back, glancing between Sage and Flint in shock. The two of them were *siblings*? They looked nothing alike.

Or at least, not at first. Besides the obvious difference of his being huge, they did have the same dark hair, tanned skin, and brown eyes. She wasn't as tall as Flint —no one in the room was as tall as Flint—but she was still taller than the average female. I supposed it wasn't completely out of the question that they could be related.

"Really?" Sage cocked her head, looking at him in challenge. "Then tell me—what *are* you doing?"

"I'm working on something," he said, darkness descending upon his gaze as he spoke. "Although it's nothing that can be shared just yet. But trust me, once it can, the pack will be the first to know. And I'll expect your unbending support in whatever my decision may be."

He held his gaze with Sage, and she stared right back, not breaking eye contact. Again with the strange staring contest thing.

Seconds passed in terse silence. Flint leaned forward and curled his lip up in a small growl, and Sage clenched her fists to her sides. I held my breath, afraid that even breathing too loudly would set the two of them off into a fight. Everyone else in the room was still as well. Sage's brow glimmered with tiny beads of sweat, like holding eye contact with her brother was causing her physical exertion. Flint looked as cool and collected as ever.

Finally, after what felt like forever, Sage lowered her gaze.

Flint leaned back in the couch and smirked, looking mighty pleased with himself.

"Fine," Sage said, flicking her eyes back up to glance at Flint. "Once you're ready to share this plan of yours, I'll listen. Until then, I hunt with Noah."

"You'll do more than listen." Flint's lip flicked up again in irritation. "You'll follow. Pack first, always."

"Pack first," Sage repeated. "That's why I'm doing my part in stopping the demons—to protect the pack. You know that."

"Very well," Flint said. "We're done here." He turned to Noah. "When will you be leaving with the human?"

"I have a name," I chimed in. I couldn't help it— despite how intimidating he was, the way Flint was speaking to everyone like he was the boss of them all was irritating me like crazy. And I hated that he was talking about me like I was an object and not a person. "Raven."

He ignored me, like I hadn't spoken at all.

"Raven and I will be leaving tomorrow," Noah said.

"Good," Flint said. "And Noah? I think it goes without saying that *the human* will be staying with you in the pool house."

With that, the pack was dismissed.

26

RAVEN

"YOU CAN TAKE THE BED," Noah said once we were back inside the pool house. "I'll sleep on the couch."

"I can take the couch." I didn't want to be more of an imposition on him than I already was. "I'm smaller than you. You should have the bed."

"No." He glared at me. "I'm taking the couch, and that's final."

A knock on the door stopped us from continuing the debate.

Noah stalked over to the door and threw it open.

Sage stood there waiting, a large stuffed bag thrown over her shoulder.

"What?" Noah glared at her with more irritation than he had at me.

"I brought some stuff over for Raven." She motioned

to the bag she was holding. "Pajamas, toothbrush, face wash, and such. I thought she'd need it after the night she just had."

I walked over to her, surprised by how thoughtful she was being. "Thanks," I said. "I appreciate it. But I thought you didn't want me here?"

"I didn't," she said. "I still don't. You're making Noah's mission more dangerous than it already is, and I won't change my mind about that. But you're doing what you need to do to save your mom, and I respect that. Plus, we're going to be spending a lot of time together in the next few weeks, so I figured this was the least I could do."

I took the bag from her, surprised by how much it weighed. What on Earth had she managed to put in there?

"Anyway, we need to get our rest for tomorrow," she continued. "So I'll be heading back to the main house now..."

"Wait," Noah said, and she paused in her tracks. "I didn't want to say anything back there—Flint would have gotten too much joy out of it if I did—but I'll understand if you decide not to come with us. I don't want to cause any more of a rift between you all than I already have."

"Don't be silly." Sage smirked. "I started this mission

with you, and I'm ending it with you, too. You know there's no changing my mind, so don't waste your breath trying."

"Wasn't planning on it," he said. "I just wanted you to know that I'd understand if you chose to stay back."

"Understood," she said. "But it doesn't matter. Especially since you're going to need my help even *more* now that Raven's tagging along."

I didn't know whether to be insulted or not. But before I could decide, she turned to me, a mischievous glint in her eyes.

"Don't be fooled by this one," she said, pointing her thumb at Noah. "He may look all rough and tough on the outside, but trust me when I say he's a big softie at heart."

She managed to wink at me right before he scowled and slammed the door shut in her face.

27

RAVEN

SAGE HAD MANAGED to stuff every amenity that a girl could ever need into that bag, and it felt amazing to shower and change after the crazy night I'd had.

I stepped out of the bathroom, in pajamas that were too big on me and my hair still wet from the shower, to find Noah sprawled out on the couch. He'd changed into sweatpants and a white t-shirt, which made him look less "supernatural demon hunter" and more "college guy living in a dorm."

But there was something about him—maybe his confidence—that made him seem ages more mature than the guys I'd shared classes with at school.

He stared at me, and I shifted in place, pulling at the sleeves of my top. The way he was looking at me made me feel more vulnerable than ever. Especially since I'd never spent the night at a guy's before. I'd had a few boyfriends in high school, but nothing that had ever gotten serious.

My face heated, and I knew I had to say something before this got more awkward than it already was.

"I haven't gotten a chance to thank you yet," I said.

"For what?" He picked up his knife from the coffee table and threw it high in the air, catching it perfectly with his other hand.

Forget what I'd thought earlier about him looking like he could pass as a college student. I didn't know any college guy who would do that.

"For saving my life in that alley," I said. "If you hadn't been there…" I didn't continue, since we both knew what would have happened if he hadn't been there.

I would have been taken, just like my mom.

"I'm no one's savior," he said. "I was just bagging my next demon tooth for my collection, and you happened to have benefited in the process."

Then he threw the knife, sending it whizzing a foot away from my face and into the center of the dartboard behind me.

"What the hell?" I jumped to the side, glaring at him. "You could have killed me!"

"You don't trust my aim?" He raised an eyebrow and stretched out on the couch, his shirt lifting to give me a peek of his perfectly defined abs. "Would you mind getting that for me?"

"Seriously?" I crossed my arms, waiting to see if he actually expected me to fetch his knife for him—the knife he'd used to scare me half to death.

He made no effort to move, which I guess meant he did.

I glanced from him to the knife and back again, and made a decision. I'd fetch his stupid knife, but I'd only hand it back once he answered one of my questions.

I stomped over for the knife and reached for it. But it burned my fingertips the moment they grazed the handle, and I shrieked, pulling my hand away.

"What?" The corner of Noah's lip quirked up in amusement. "Never touched a knife before?"

"That's not just any knife!" I examined the pads of my fingers. They were red, but it wasn't too bad. If I hadn't pulled away so quickly, it would have been much worse. "It was as hot as a stove on the highest setting."

"Interesting." He got up, walked up to the knife, and easily pulled it out of the dartboard. "I guess heavenly weapons are too powerful for humans to handle."

"So you didn't know it would do that to me?" I asked.

"What?" He stood perfectly still, tilting his head as he gazed down at me. "You thought I was trying to burn your hand?"

I raised an eyebrow, saying nothing.

"I wasn't trying to burn you," he said. "That would make you even more of a burden than you already are."

The harshness of his words made me freeze in place. "Are you going to be like this the whole time we're traveling together?" I asked. "Because it's going to get old real fast."

"I didn't say anything that wasn't true." He shrugged.

I wanted to stomp off into the bedroom, slam the door in his face, and not talk to him for the rest of the night. But I had too many questions, and he was the only one around who could answer them.

So for now, I was staying put.

"What's a heavenly weapon?" I asked, glancing at the knife in his hand. It was silver, but beyond that, it didn't look like anything special.

"It's a weapon that an angel has dipped in heavenly water." He examined the knife as he returned to the couch. "Heavenly weapons are the only weapons that can kill demons."

That was the longest answer I'd gotten from him so far. I walked over to the armchair and situated myself in it, ready to finally get all my questions out in the open.

"By 'killing them,' you mean 'turn them into pile of ash,'" I said. "Right? Like I saw in the alley?"

"Yeah." Apparently he was back to one-word answers.

But I wasn't going to let that stop me from asking my questions.

"And you and Sage—and the rest of the 'pack' in the house—can do this because you're demon hunters?" I searched my mind for the specific word Rosella had used back at the Pier. "Nephilim?"

"That's enough of the questions," he said. "It's been a long night, and we both have to get some sleep to be ready for what's coming tomorrow."

"I answered your questions earlier." I crossed my arms, not bothering to hide my irritation. "Now it's your turn to answer mine."

"It's three in the morning," he said.

"So?"

"First rule of demon hunting—if it's convenient to grab sleep, do it," he said. "You need to store up as much energy as possible, and there's no saying when you'll be able to sleep next. Being awake and on your game when it counts the most could be the difference between ending up alive or dead." He rammed the tip of his knife into the coffee table, as if making a point. There were lots of matching little dots on the surface—I supposed he did that a lot.

"I'm too wired up to sleep." I crossed one leg over the other, making myself comfortable.

"You're overtired," he said. "Big difference."

"Or *you're* purposefully avoiding telling me what you, Sage, and the rest of the 'pack' inside that house really are."

He pressed his lips together and took a deep breath, like he was about to say something mean but was stopping himself. "You're about to join me and Sage on a mission to kill four more demons," he said. "Trust me—there will be plenty of time on the road for you to ask all the questions you want. For now, you need sleep."

I leaned back, frustration rushing through my veins. He was trying to distract me. But I refused to let him succeed.

"You're not a Nephilim, are you?" I asked.

"What makes you think that?"

I matched his gaze with mine, wanting to show him that I wasn't going to back down. "Because every time I ask, you change the subject."

He was silent for a few seconds, and I leaned forward, prepared to *finally* get an answer.

"Tell you what," he said. "Go lay down on the bed, turn off the lights, and close your eyes. Stay like that for ten minutes."

"And then what?" I asked.

"Then you'll fall asleep."

"And if I don't?"

"Then come back out here and we'll talk," he said. "But it has to be ten minutes. I'll be timing you."

"Fine." I stood up and marched to the bedroom. "See you in ten minutes."

Noah followed behind me.

I spun around my heel to face him. He must not have been expecting it, because he ran straight into me. I stumbled, and he reached for my wrists to steady me.

"What are you doing?" he asked.

"That's funny," I said. "I was about to ask you the exact same thing." My wrists heated under his touch, and I swallowed, every cell in my body suddenly aware of how there were only inches between my body and his.

"I'm making sure you actually get into the bed and turn off the lights." His eyes were intense as they gazed into mine, and he spoke slower, as if trying to hypnotize me with his voice. Electricity sizzled in the air between us, and I found myself at a loss for words.

Was he doing this on purpose to make me comply? Because I refused to let my attraction to him distract me. I had more important things to worry about—like saving my mom.

"You don't trust me?" I pulled my wrists out of his

grasp and stepped back, breaking whatever connection I thought there'd been between us.

"Regarding this?" He smirked, back to his typical couldn't care less attitude. "Absolutely not."

I said nothing, because he was right—I had no intention of doing as he'd asked and risking falling asleep. But now I had no other choice.

So I got into the bed and under the covers. The mattress was surprisingly soft. I also couldn't help noticing that the covers smelled warm and woodsy, like Noah.

He stood in the doorframe and watched as I tucked myself in. Not in a creepy way—it was more like how a parent would watch a kid to make sure they were obeying their bedtime.

It was condescending, to say the least. So I glared at him, wanting him to know exactly how I felt about the way he was acting.

Once I rested my head on the pillow, he smiled and flicked off the lights.

He must have been right that I was tired.

Because despite my desire to learn more about Noah and the entire supernatural world he'd dragged me into, my eyelids drooped shut and I fell asleep in seconds.

28

RAVEN

I WAS IN A DARK CELL—THE only light came from a candle flickering somewhere nearby. It was dark and musty, and my mouth tasted like sandpaper. But I screamed and screamed to be let out, my hands gripping the bars in desperation.

"Stop that screaming," a woman said from across the way. She was movie star gorgeous, and was wearing a tight sparkly dress that looked more fit for a club than a dirty jail cell. "Don't you know by now that no one can hear you?"

"You don't know that," I said. "We have to at least try. They have to know we're here if we want any chance of being rescued."

"My family will find me and rescue me." She sounded pretty snobby for someone in the same exact situation as me. "But your screaming won't help, so you might as well save your breath."

Maybe she was right, but I refused to sit around and do nothing. So I gripped the bars tighter and screamed for help again.

Suddenly, someone appeared in the hall between the cells. A short woman in a fringe dress that looked like it came from another era, her hair styled in a flapper bob. "Stephenie's right," she said with a menacing smile. "Not that her family will rescue you, because they don't even know she's gone. But she's right that there's no point in screaming. This entire prison is soundproof. All you're doing is exhausting yourself and giving the others a headache."

She raised something in the air—a dart gun—and I screamed again as she shot a dart straight into my neck.

BRIGHTNESS FILLED THE ROOM, and my eyes shot open.

My heart raced. I could still hear the screams lingering in my mind. My hand rushed to my neck, but nothing was there. And the dream—nightmare—was already fading. But I could still recall the sheer terror and helplessness that it had made me feel. I didn't think I'd ever forget it.

Now the lights were on in the room, and Noah was standing in the doorway. Even though he was still in his pajamas, he was on full alert, looking around the room as if a monster could be hiding around any corner.

Had I just screamed in my sleep?

How embarrassing.

I sat up and rubbed the sleep out of my eyes. "What time is it?" I asked groggily, trying to break the awkward silence between us.

"I heard you screaming." He shuffled his feet, barely meeting my eyes. "I thought Azazel had found you."

"Azazel?" I asked, still in a daze after the nightmare.

"The greater demon," he said. "The older man in the alley in the leather jacket. The one who took your mom."

"Right." My heart dropped at the reminder that my mom was missing. "No demon. It was just a nightmare. Sorry for waking you up."

"It's past noon." He ran a hand through his perfectly tousled hair. "You didn't wake me up."

I glanced at the window—sure enough, light peeked through the blinds.

He walked over and opened them, letting the natural sunlight flow into the room.

"Did I really sleep for over ten hours?" I asked.

"Yep," he said. "Told you that you needed sleep."

"I guess." I shrugged, not wanting to give him the satisfaction of saying he was right.

Suddenly, the front door banged open, and Sage

rushed inside. She was already dressed and ready for the day, and she held up a knife, looking ready to fight.

"Is everything all right in here?" Her eyes scanned the room, and she relaxed at the realization that there was no imminent danger. "Sorry," she said. "I heard Raven screaming..."

"You heard all the way from the house?" I groaned, burying my face in my hands.

"Enhanced hearing." She pointed to one of her ears.

"Everything's fine." Noah's voice was terse. "Raven was just having a nightmare."

My cheeks flushed, since something about the way he said it made me sound like a little kid. "After everything I went through last night, can you blame me?" I asked.

"What you saw last night was *nothing* compared to the horrors that are out there," he said. "Are you sure you're up for all of this?"

"I'm sure," I said, although my voice wavered.

How could I ever be prepared for the terrors to come? The truth was that I wanted no part in any of this.

But with my mom abducted, I had no choice.

"I'm coming with you." I forced confidence into my tone. "Stop trying to talk me out of it."

"I wasn't trying to talk you out of it," he said. "I was just trying to give you the facts."

"Would you guys cut the crap?" Sage crossed her arms and glared at both of us. "Because I'm hungry, and we have a mission to start."

29

RAVEN

SAGE MANAGED to find jeans and a tank that fit me decently, although I had to roll up the bottoms of the jeans to keep them from bunching up. She brought us some food from the main house—a variety of bacon, ham, and sausage. It looked like enough for six people, not three.

My mom would have had a fit at the all-meat meal. Tears filled my eyes at the thought of her, but I wolfed down the food anyway, more determined than ever to get started.

"Where are we heading?" I asked once I'd had my fill. Sage and Noah were still chowing down—the amount of food they were consuming was strangely impressive.

"We have some witch contacts in Beverly Hills," Noah said after polishing off a piece of bacon. "They can use a tracking spell to locate the next demon for us to hunt."

"There are witches in Beverly Hills?" I didn't know what I'd expected him to say, but it certainly hadn't been *that*.

"Not just any witches," Sage chimed in. "The Devereux witches are the most powerful witches in all of California."

"And they live in Beverly Hills." I chuckled. "The same neighborhood as my grandparents."

"Really?" Sage looked at me quizzically. "You didn't strike me as the rich girl type."

"My mom's always forged her own path, but a store and apartment in Venice Beach isn't cheap," I explained. "The initial investment had to come from somewhere."

"Makes sense," Noah said, and then he re-focused on the food, continuing to inhale more food in one sitting than I thought was humanly possible.

Which I supposed shouldn't have been strange, since he *wasn't* a human.

"So, the two of you aren't Nephilim, you aren't witches, and seeing as you didn't combust in the sunlight, I guess you're not vampires either." I rested my elbows on the table, studying each of them. They were too focused on their food to notice. "Since we're all here, now seems like a good time for you to enlighten me on what you *really* are."

Sage nearly choked on a sausage. "You haven't told her?" she asked Noah.

"It was late last night," he said. "She needed sleep."

"Now I've gotten that sleep," I said. "And since we're going to be demon hunting together for the foreseeable future, it's only fair that you're honest with me about what you are."

"Fine." Noah looked at me pointedly. "But firstly, you should know that vampires don't combust in the sunlight."

"So you're vampires?" I studied both of them, my gaze lowering to the food on their plates. "But you're eating food. I thought vampires could only drink blood."

"Vampires only need blood to survive, but they can still eat food for enjoyment," Sage said. "But you were right before—we're not vampires."

"All right," I said. "So what are you?"

"We're shifters," Noah said simply. "More specifically, wolf shifters."

I looked at him and Sage, trying to take in what he'd said. I guessed "wolf shifter" meant they could shift into wolves. I supposed the speed, the sense of smell, calling their family a "pack," and their love for meat made sense with that. But there was one thing that *didn't* make sense.

"So you can shift… into wolves," I started, the words sounding absurd as I spoke them out loud. "But you weren't wolves when you fought the demon. You looked the same as you look now. Like humans."

"We can't fight demons in wolf form," Noah said. "Well, we could fight them, but we couldn't kill them. Demons can only be killed with a heavenly weapon. It's much easier to wield a weapon in human form than wolf form. Opposable thumbs are useful for holding weapons."

"But if we have to fight any other kind of creature, we shift," Sage added. "Our teeth and claws are our deadliest weapons of all." She smiled to show off her perfect teeth, as if proving her point.

"If our teeth and claws could be turned into heavenly weapons, we'd be a force to be reckoned with," Noah said.

"Like Wolverine," I said, trying my best to make light of all this craziness.

"Who?" Noah cocked his head, looking genuinely confused.

"Wolverine," I said, slower this time. "From the *X-Men* movies?"

He watched me blankly, like I was speaking another language.

"You've never heard of *X-Men?*" My eyes widened—he couldn't be serious.

He said nothing. Apparently, he *was* being serious.

"Have you been living under a rock for your whole life?" I asked. "I mean, I'd get it if you haven't ever *seen* one of the *X-Men* movies, but to have never *heard* of them? That's crazy."

"I'm not from around here." He stared at me, and I closed my mouth, getting a feeling that if I said one more word he was going to blow a fuse.

"Sorry." I pulled at a piece of bacon on my plate, even though I was full. "I wasn't saying it to be insulting."

"I'm not *insulted.*" He sneered, as if the possibility of being insulted by someone like me—by a *human*—disgusted him.

"All right then." I turned to Sage, hoping she'd be more open to answering my questions. "The others in the main house—they're wolves too, aren't they?" I asked.

"Yep," she said. "We're all members of the Montgomery pack—the most powerful shifter pack in California."

"By that, she means the *richest,*" Noah said, and I gave him a small smile, hoping that his entrance back into the conversation meant that the awkward disagreement before was forgotten.

"My brother—Flint—is our alpha," Sage continued. "I'm the beta, which means other than Flint, the rest of them submit to whatever I want."

"Including Noah?" I raised an eyebrow at him. Even though Sage was a badass, I couldn't see him submitting to *anyone*.

"No." He sat straighter, serious again. "I'm not part of the Montgomery pack."

"Oh," I said, although I felt stupid the minute after, since I should have figured as much. If he wasn't from here, it made sense that he wouldn't be in the pack. "So, where's your pack?"

His eyes darkened. "I don't have a pack," he said.

I wanted to ask more—to ask what happened to his pack—but something about his expression made me stop. Whatever had happened must have been bad. And I was finally getting answers from him. The last thing I wanted was for him to shut down again.

Still, the more I learned about Noah, the more curious I was about his past.

"Noah's a guest here," Sage explained, breaking the awkward silence that had descended upon the room again. "As long as he respects Flint, he's not bound to our chain of command."

I opened my mouth to ask my next question, but Noah spoke first.

"Are you done?" he asked Sage, glancing at her empty plate.

"Yeah," she said.

"Good." Ignoring me, he walked over to the coffee table and retrieved his knife, shoving it inside a pocket in his jacket. "Because we've answered enough questions for one morning. It's time we hit the road."

RAVEN

I FINALLY HAD a chance to collect my thoughts on the ride to Beverly Hills, and the first people I wondered about were my grandparents. Since I'd called the police last night before disappearing with Noah and Sage, the cops must have arrived to an empty apartment.

What did they think had happened? The only logical thought process was that I'd been abducted by the same person who'd taken my mom—especially since my phone had been left behind. Surely the cops had notified my grandparents by now?

They must be so worried.

Once we were back at the Montgomery compound, I'd figure out a way to contact them to let them know that I was okay. But what would I tell them about Mom? I couldn't tell them the truth. I also couldn't lie and say she was fine—they'd realize once she wasn't there to speak with them that she was gone, and they'd want answers. They'd go to the cops. But obviously the cops couldn't get involved, given how this was a supernatural problem—not a human problem.

I had no idea what to tell them. Hopefully Noah and Sage would be able to advise me on the best course of action.

Eventually, we pulled up to a mansion three times the size of the one my grandparents lived in. It had to have been the biggest on the block—if not one of the biggest in all of Beverly Hills.

"One more thing," Sage said to me as she got off her bike. "Last night, one of the witches in their circle was killed by Azazel. If the sisters seem upset, that's why."

"Oh no," I said. "That's awful."

"I doubt the witches will be thrilled that you're here, so just stay quiet and let us do the talking." Noah hopped off the bike and turned to me. "Is that something you're even capable of doing?"

"Of course I am." Irritation coursed through me at the way he was talking down to me again. He'd already made it clear last night that he thought I was a burden. There was no need to treat me like crap on top of it.

But he also had a point—sometimes I had a hard time keeping my mouth shut.

"At least, I can try," I added.

"Good." He held out a hand, and I stared at it, unsure what he was doing.

Was he helping me off the bike?

It sure seemed like it. Which was strange, because he hadn't helped me off the bike any of the other times that I'd ridden with him.

Sage raised an eyebrow, but she said nothing.

Not wanting to make a big deal about it, I lowered my hand into his, allowing him to help me down.

His skin was warm to the touch. Was that a wolf shifter thing, or a Noah thing? I didn't know. I had *so* many more questions for him, but obviously now wasn't the time. So I just gave him a small smile in thanks before running my fingers through my hair in an attempt to have something to do with my hand after removing it from his.

He turned around and headed toward the door, as if not wanting to acknowledge that he'd helped me at all. He knocked, and the door opened seconds later.

A petite blonde who looked around my age stood inside. She wore a cotton tracksuit, and her eyes were red and puffy, as if she'd been crying.

"Amber," Noah said her name warmly. "Thanks for seeing us on such short notice."

"I have your potion ready," she said. Then she looked

past him, straight at me. Her eyes flicked to Sage's ring on my finger and filled with suspicion. "Who's your friend?" she asked, turning back to Noah.

I almost introduced myself. But then I remembered what Noah had said about staying quiet, so I pressed my lips together, saying nothing.

"Raven's a human," Noah said. "She lives in the apartment above Tarotology."

"You were able to get to her before Azazel?" she asked. "And you're all still in one piece? How…?" She looked back and forth between Noah and Sage, her mouth open in shock and confusion.

"Azazel had already been to the apartment by the time I got home," I told Amber. "He took my mom."

Noah glanced over his shoulder and glared at me.

I almost asked him what the look was about, but then I remembered—he'd asked me to let him and Sage do all the talking.

I *really* wasn't good at the whole staying quiet thing.

"I'm sorry for your loss." Amber lowered her eyes, and I had a feeling that she was thinking of the sister she'd lost last night.

"Yours, too." Screw that not talking thing. Amber didn't seem to be offended by the fact that I was speaking to her, and I wasn't just going to stand here and act like I didn't exist. "But my mom's not dead. Azazel took her, but she's still alive."

Amber tilted her head, looking at me quizzically. "How do you know all of this?" she asked.

"It's a long story," Noah said. "One that *Sage and I* will tell you once we're inside." He turned slightly in my direction while saying that final part, as if reminding me that I was supposed to let the two of them do the talking.

I nodded to let him know the message was received.

I didn't like it, but this was only day one of our mission, and I didn't want to continue on a worse foot than we'd already started on.

"I can't wait to hear it." Amber opened the door wider, watching me with interest as the three of us entered the mansion.

RAVEN

AMBER'S SISTERS, Bella, Evangeline, and Doreen, joined us in the living room. The women looked nothing alike. I figured they weren't biological sisters, but that they called each other sisters because they were in the same witch circle.

Their house was clean and pristine... except for an area stained red near the steps. A shiver ran down my spine at the sight of it. It looked like blood.

Had their sister been killed here, in the house? Was that her blood?

I wanted to ask, but even I knew that would seriously be crossing a line.

Once we were all situated on the couches, Noah and Sage caught the witches up on everything that had happened since they'd found me in the apartment.

"You really stabbed Sage in the shoulder?" Evangeline asked me once they were done. "With a *crystal wand?*"

"It was the only object in my room that could double as a weapon." I shrugged.

"Smart." She smiled. "I like you."

"Thanks." I smiled in return.

At least *one* of the supernaturals in the room had taken a liking to me.

"Anyway," Sage said, and the witches refocused on her. "We're here because we need a scrying spell to find the next demon."

"No more staying close and waiting for them to appear in nearby cities," Noah added. "We need to get to Avalon as soon as possible. So if the only active demon is all the way across the country, then we'll go all the way across the country."

"Are you sure?" Sage asked. "The Montgomery pack's strongest allies are on the West coast. If we venture farther out, we'll lose that safety net."

"I'm sure," Noah said. "The demons *have* to be abducting these humans for a reason, and whatever the reason is can't be good. The sooner I get to Avalon, the sooner I can join the Earth Angel's army and start making a real difference in this war."

"And the sooner we get to Avalon, the sooner I can start the Angel Trials so I can save my mom," I added.

"You don't even know what the Angel Trials are," Sage said.

"And you do?"

"I've heard things." Her eyes flickered with hesitation, and she leaned back in her seat, not looking willing to share. "It's supposed to be pretty dangerous."

"That's why I'm coming with you on the hunt." I sat straight, refusing to back down. "So that I'm prepared for whatever these trials entail."

"Enough jabbering," Amber said, and all eyes in the room went to her. "You can discuss the Angel Trials on your own time. Right now, we have business to attend to."

"Right," Noah said. "The scrying spell to find the next demon."

"We'll get to that," she said. "But first things first—the potion I promised you yesterday is ready."

"What potion?" I asked.

"As you know, Azazel is a greater demon, so Sage and Noah can't kill him—not even with a heavenly weapon," she said.

"Right," I said, since I'd learned all of this already. "Only Nephilim can kill greater demons."

"Exactly," she said. "Which makes the three of you

helpless against Azazel if he shows up. But my sisters and I stayed up for hours last night trying to figure out something that would allow you to defend yourselves. I think you'll be pleased with the result."

"And?" Noah tapped his foot, clearly running out of patience. "What is it?"

"A potion that if administered to a supernatural with teleportation abilities, will send them back to the last place they jumped from and will leave them unable to jump again for five minutes," she said. "Those five minutes should allow you enough time to run to safety."

"Perfect." Sage smiled mischievously. "I always love a new potion for the dart gun."

My hand instinctively went to my neck. At the mention of a dart gun, I'd suddenly remembered the way my nightmare last night had ended—with someone shooting a dart straight into my neck. Of course, the skin there was fine. But the coincidence of dreaming about a dart gun and then having one pop into conversation today was strange.

"The potion is pretty old school," Evangeline said. "We had to pore over dusty books for hours last night before finding it. And the ingredients needed for it were rare."

"They were." Bella spoke for the first time since introducing herself. "Luckily it wasn't dark magic, and we're also invested in stopping Azazel, so the potion plus the scrying spell will be only twenty grand."

My mouth dropped open at the high cost. *Twenty grand* for a few hours worth of work?

If that was the cost of a light magic spell, how much could the dark magic spells cost?

No wonder the witches were able to afford a mansion in Beverly Hills.

"No problem." Sage whipped out a black credit card and handed it to Amber, who ran it through a little swipe machine attached to her phone.

"Perfect," Amber said, returning the card to Sage. "Now, who's ready to scry for a demon?"

RAVEN

AMBER LED NOAH, Sage, and me into a room she called her *apothecary*. Her sisters stayed behind.

The apothecary was the size of a den, with no windows and shelves full of plants and potions lining the walls. I imagined that the person who'd originally built the house had intended for it to be a home theatre of sorts.

"Your sisters don't need to help with the scrying spell?" I asked.

"Nope," Amber said. "Scrying spells are light magic. My sisters all practice dark magic. Whitney was a light magic witch, but since Azazel murdered her, now it's just me." Her eyes flared with grief and anger at the mention of her fallen sister.

I had no idea what to say—I'd never lost anyone close to me—so I stayed quiet.

Amber gathered the necessary materials—an atlas that she spread out on the center table, four differently colored candles, and a pendulum with a crystal on the end.

My mom sold pendulums at the store and had a few of them around the house, but they never seemed to do anything.

I supposed that wasn't the case when an *actual* witch was doing the spell.

After lighting the candles, Amber held out her hand to Noah. He reached inside his jacket, pulled out his knife, and handed it to her. The knife didn't burn her like it had burned me.

Noah must have been right that it had burned me because I was human.

Amber muttered a few words I didn't understand, and the pendulum started to swing. I looked at her fingers to check if she were making it swing or not—my mom had been known to do that whenever she used pendulums—but Amber's fingers were perfectly still.

The pendulum was swinging on its own.

It led her hand across the map, and Sage, Noah, and I leaned forward to watch. It was going east.

Eventually, the pendulum stopped swinging—right over the lower half of Louisiana.

"I've found your next demon," Amber said, the flames from the candles reflecting in her eyes. "In the heart of New Orleans."

RAVEN

"It looks like we're going on a road trip," Noah said.

"I've never been to New Orleans." Sage rubbed her hands together—I couldn't tell if she was excited or nervous. "The Montgomery pack isn't allied with the rougarou, so the city's always been off-limits."

"The rougarou?" I raised an eyebrow in question.

"The wolf shifters who live around New Orleans," she said. "They're Cajun French, so they call themselves by their French name. They dominate the New Orleans area, and they don't take kindly to visits from other shifters."

"Then it's a good thing we have our cloaking rings," Noah said. "We'll be in and out of the city with the rougarou never the wiser."

"And luckily for the three of you, New Orleans is a

hot spot for witches," Amber said. "I have a contact for the most powerful witch circle there. I'll text you her information."

"Great," Sage said. "And again, I really am sorry about Whitney."

"Thanks." Amber sniffed and rubbed at her eyes. "Azazel was…" She paused, as if unable to put her feelings into words. "He was terrifying. I hope the Earth Angel's army is able to stop the demons. If they can't…" She trailed off, the possibilities of the destruction the demons could cause lingering in the air.

"Annika's army *will* stop the demons." Noah sounded absolutely sure of it. His unwavering faith in the Earth Angel was clear every time he spoke of her.

What kind of history was there between them that made him admire her so much?

"I'm sure she'll welcome you to Avalon, if you're interested in joining to do as much as you can to help," he said.

"I'd been considering it." She twisted a strand of hair around her finger. "But Whitney used her Final Spell to strengthen the boundary around the house. Not even greater demons can get past it now. And I refuse to let her Final Spell have been in vain. My place is here. But I *am* hoping to make an alliance with Annika—one that will involve my sisters and I staying home, where we belong, and offering whatever support the army needs."

"From what Noah says about Annika, I'm sure she'll appreciate it," Sage said. "But now that we have the potion to use against greater demons and the location of the next demon for our hunt, there's no time to waste. We need to get to New Orleans as soon as possible."

"Of course," Amber said, turning to me. "But there's one more thing I wanted to give you."

"Me?" I asked. What could the witch possibly have to give to me?

She didn't even know I *existed* until I came over here with Noah and Sage.

She reached into her pocket and pulled out something I'd recognize anywhere—my mom's lapis lazuli necklace.

"How do you have that?" I eyed Amber suspiciously, glancing back and forth between her and the necklace.

"Azazel brought it here last night." She looked down at the necklace as she spoke, unable to meet my gaze. "He wanted me to track its owner."

I was speechless as the pieces of the puzzle shifted into place. "You did it, didn't you?" I clenched my fists, anger rushing through my veins. "You did a scrying spell for her like you did for the demon in New Orleans, and you told him where she was. *That's* how he knew to go to the store to begin with."

"I'm so sorry." Her lower lip trembled—she sounded like she was about to cry. "I didn't want to do it. But he killed Whitney, and he was going to kill my other sisters if I didn't do as he said. I had no choice."

"There's always a choice." I snatched the necklace out of her hand, unable to look at her.

If she hadn't told Azazel where to find my mom, my mom would still be home today.

But was it really fair to blame Amber? After all, if I hadn't been wearing the necklace last night, my mom would still be here today too. If I hadn't gone out last night at *all*, I never would have met Eli and gotten involved in this whole mess in the first place. So really, if anyone was to blame for my mom's abduction, it was myself.

But that wasn't fair either.

Because the only person responsible for my mom's abduction was *Azazel*.

"I'm sorry." I looked her straight in the eye so she'd know I meant it. "I know it wasn't your fault. If Azazel had been threatening to kill my mom or someone else I loved, I would have done what he'd asked, too. I can't blame you for protecting your family."

"Thank you for understanding," she said. "I really do hope you're able to get your mom back."

"Can you use the necklace to scry for her?" I asked, hope blooming in my chest. "You were able to scry for her before, so you should be able to now. Right?"

"I can't." She hung her head, looking defeated. "I tried last night—I thought that if Azazel had taken your mom, I might be able to use the necklace to track him, too. But I should've known better. Azazel wouldn't have left the necklace here if he'd thought I'd be able to use it to track him. Wherever he brought your mom is guarded with a powerful cloaking spell. When I tried to scry for her, I hit a wall. It's too powerful to break through. I'm sorry."

I deflated. Just when I thought there might have been hope, it was ripped away from me.

"Thanks for trying," I said, although the words felt hollow as I spoke them.

But I needed to get ahold of myself. So I fastened the necklace back on my neck, hoping the stone would bring me the strength my mom believed it would. Because all wasn't lost. I could still save my mom. I just needed to focus on what I *could* do.

Which was helping Noah hunt down his final four demons, getting to Avalon, and participating in the Angel Trials.

"So, are you guys ready to hit the road?" I asked

Noah and Sage, trying to infuse as much confidence into my tone as possible. "Because there's a demon in New Orleans waiting for you to put that magic knife of yours straight through its heart so you can add its tooth to your collection."

34

RAVEN

WE HEADED BACK to the compound so that Sage and Noah could pack.

Once in the pool house, Noah took out a suitcase and started haphazardly throwing an array of clothing in there. His clothes were pretty much identical—jeans and t-shirts in both solid black and white. No other colors, no other patterns, no other designs.

Nothing that might give any clue of his personality. It was like he'd bulk ordered everything and called it a day.

Although I supposed that was better than my situation, seeing as everything I owned was in a pile in his room. Even the clothes I was wearing now belonged to Sage.

"Do you think we could stop by my apartment when

we leave?" I asked. "I'd like to get some of my clothes. And my phone."

I couldn't remember a time when I'd *ever* gone this long without checking my phone. We'd been so busy that I hadn't even had the time to think of it, but I surely had tons of worried messages by now.

Noah's head shot up, his eyes alarmed. "Absolutely not," he said. "Your apartment is a crime scene now. You can't go back there."

"Then what am I supposed to wear?" I asked. "I have no clothes."

"Sage can lend you more of hers." He returned to packing, as if that answer was supposed to have satisfied me.

"Fine," I said. "But if I can't get my phone, can I borrow yours? I need to get in touch with my grandparents and friends to let them know I'm okay."

"Are you crazy?" He slammed his suitcase shut and stood, towering over me with a menacing scowl. "You can't let *anyone* know where you are. Don't you understand that by now?"

"I wasn't going to let them know where I am," I said, since clearly *that* would be stupid. "I just wanted them to know I'm okay. So they won't worry."

"And what exactly do you plan on telling them?" He crossed his arms in challenge. "That you're tagging along with two wolf shifters on a journey halfway across the country to kill a demon?"

"Of course not." I scoffed. "I'd just say I was going on a cross country trip and not to worry about me. After what happened with Europe over the winter, I doubt anyone would be surprised."

"What happened with Europe over the winter?" he asked.

"I went there on a backpacking trip without telling anyone." I shrugged.

"Why?"

"I don't know." I picked at my cuticles, the same unsettled feeling coming over me that I experienced whenever the topic of my trip to Europe came up.

It was a feeling of emptiness, like something I was saying wasn't *right*.

"You jetted off to Europe for the winter and don't know why?" He smirked and raised an eyebrow. "Sounds like I'm not the only one with secrets."

"Whatever," I said, not wanting to continue this conversation further. "The point is that they'll believe my story."

"And *my* point is that you can't communicate with them at all." He stepped closer—so close that I could smell the now-familiar woodsy scent that seemed to constantly emanate off his skin. "Unless you want to risk putting them in danger?"

"Why would them knowing I was safe be putting them in danger?" I tried to keep my voice steady, despite how my heart was pounding due to his close proximity to me. I took a step back, but I hit the wall, unable to go far.

"Because you're *not* safe," he said. "You're involved in the supernatural world, and you're coming with me and Sage to hunt demons. The less your friends and family know, the better."

"So what?" I threw my hands up in frustration. "I'm supposed to let them think I'm missing? That my mom's missing?"

"Your mom *is* missing," he said.

"But I'm not."

"To them, you are."

We stood at a standstill, neither of us backing down.

"No one can know where you are or what you're doing." He spoke softer now, as if *maybe* he empathized with my feelings. "I know it's hard, but you have to cut contact. It's what's best for them." His eyes went distant at the last part. Was he thinking about this situation or about something else—like the reason why he was a lone wolf?

"Fine," I said, since the last thing I wanted to do was

endanger my family or friends. "But the cops know something happened. They got my 911 call. They're going to be looking for me and my mom."

"They won't find anything," he said. "The supernatural world is adept at covering our tracks. You'll just be two more missing person cases. That's all."

"You make it sound like it happens all the time," I said.

"It does."

"Well, that sounds... scary." I shivered, wondering how much crime was caused naturally, and how much was supernatural.

"It *is* scary." His voice was stronger now—harsher— and I stepped back so my back was pressed against the wall. "This is *all* scary. *We're* scary. Haven't you seen enough of my world by now to realize that?"

"You're not scary." The words slipped out of my mouth before I realized it.

"You know nothing about me." He smirked and backed away. "You wouldn't think that if you did."

"I know you saved my life, and that you're helping me save my mom's," I said. "I trust you. Although now that you mention it, I *do* have more questions. Mainly about what you are and what you can do."

"You can say it." He ambled toward me, his eyes glimmering in challenge. "I won't bite."

"Werewolf," I whispered, since the predatory way he was watching me *was* slightly scary. But I meant it that I trusted him, so I got ahold of myself, not wanting him to think he intimidated me. "I have questions about what it's like to be a werewolf."

He stopped when there was only a foot between us, saying nothing. He just watched me with such intensity that I felt like I was being observed under a microscope.

I swallowed, staying quiet in fear that if I spoke, he'd shut down on me again.

The silence stretched out between us. Then he reached forward and pressed his palm to the wall, his arm nearly brushing my shoulder.

He was so close that he took my breath away. But I tilted my head up to meet his gaze, wanting him to see that I was ready for whatever he'd throw at me. I wouldn't back down.

"First of all, *werewolves* don't exist," he said. "Werewolves—creatures who are slaves to the full moon—are from mythology. I'm a shifter. Specifically, a wolf shifter."

"Okay." I steadied myself, trying to stay focused. Was it just me, or was he trying to distract me from asking questions by standing so close to me?

If that's what he was doing, I wasn't going to let him win.

"So you can shift at will." I kept my gaze steady, reining in my focus.

"Yes," he said. "Although we stay in human form as much as possible."

"Why?"

He tilted his head so he was even closer to me. His breath smelled of cinnamon, and I leaned forward as I waited for his answer, until our noses were almost touching.

Why was he having such a tantalizing affect on me?

"The more time we spend in human form, the easier it is to hold onto our humanity." His pupils dilated as he gazed down at me—apparently I wasn't the only one affected by our close proximity. "So we only shift into wolf form when it's necessary."

"What happens if you stay in your wolf form for too long?" I asked.

"You don't want to know." He pressed his other hand against the wall, so he was caging me in.

"Yes I do." I lifted my chin, annoyed that he was telling me what I should and shouldn't want to know. "That's why I'm asking."

His breathing slowed, and I could have sworn that his eyes dropped down to look at my lips before turning back to meet my gaze again. "I meant that you might not like the answer," he said.

"That doesn't change the fact that I want to know." My heart pounded so quickly that I wondered if he could hear it.

He likely could hear it. After all, he *did* have enhanced senses.

From the intense way he was watching me, I wasn't sure if he was about to shut down, answer my question, or kiss me.

I hoped it was the latter.

Then I chided myself for giving into his temptation. Because I needed *answers*—I didn't need to lose my focus because of Noah's attempts at distracting me.

That was all he was doing—distracting me. Because there was no way he was actually *interested* in me. Right?

From the way he was looking at me, I couldn't be sure.

Suddenly, someone knocked on the door.

I flinched at the interruption.

"It's Sage," Noah muttered, his eyes flickering with irritation. Then the side of his lip curled up mischievously. "If you want to continue this conversation, we could always tell her that we're not here..." he said.

"You know I can hear you!" Sage screamed through the door and pounded on it again. Then she barged in, her eyes widening when she saw how close Noah and I were standing. "Looks like a very interesting... conversation." She said the last word slower, clearly not believing that was what had been going on in here.

"It was." I ducked under Noah's arm and turned to face Sage. My face heated—I imagined it was so red right now that if I looked back at Noah, he'd instantly realize the affect he'd had on me. "I was learning more about werewolves. I mean *shifters*. Since werewolves don't exist."

"They don't exist in this realm." She shrugged. "As for the other realms, who knows?"

"Other *realms*?" I repeated. "And here I thought that this world was the only one I had to deal with."

"We don't have access to the other realms, so this one *is* the only one we need to deal with," she said. "But that's not why I came over right now."

"Oh?" Noah stepped up to stand next to me and draped one of his arms over my shoulders. My entire body warmed at his touch. "Because Raven and I were having a very interesting... *conversation*."

I shrugged out from under his arm, not in the mood to be toyed with—now, or *ever*. "It wasn't like that," I said, even though I couldn't help but wonder what would have happened if Sage hadn't barged in when she did. "Anyway, what's up?" I tried to sound cool and collected, even though I'd never felt so far from it in my life.

"I figured you might want to come with me to my room to see which of my clothes fit you," she said. "Unless you plan on wearing the same outfit for the entire trip?"

"Great!" I said. Then I cleared my throat, since I'd sounded way too perky. "I mean, yes. That sounds good."

"Perfect," she said. "Come on."

Somehow, I managed not to longingly glance back at Noah as I followed her out of the pool house.

RAVEN

SAGE'S ROOM was on the first floor, with a door that led
to the backyard so we were able to get inside without
running into any other members of the Montgomery
pack. It was huge, with a canopy bed, crystal chandelier,
and a fluffy pastel pink rug in the center.

I didn't know what I'd expected her room to look
like, but it certainly hadn't been something so girly.

"Won't the others hear me in here?" I whispered once
she'd closed the door. "They were pretty clear about
wanting me to stay in the pool house and out of the
main house."

"We all have sound proof spells around our rooms,
for privacy," she said. "It would get *really* annoying to
live in the same house otherwise." She rolled her eyes
and chuckled.

MICHELLE MADOW

"But you were able to hear me scream this morning in Noah's room," I said.

"Noah's not pack," she said. "The pool house is for guests, so it doesn't have a sound proof spell."

"How far *can* you hear?" I asked. "You heard me scream, so can you hear anything else?"

"Like what?" She waggled her eyebrows.

"Nothing like that." I laughed nervously, and I had a sinking feeling that my cheeks were turning red again. "Can you hear our regular conversations?"

"Our hearing's good, but not *that* good." She ran her eyes up and down my body, as if sizing me up. "I think I've got some old stuff that'll fit you," she said, walking over to the closet and swinging the door open. It was a walk-in so large that it was nearly the same size as the single rooms in the dorms at school.

"Wow," I said. "If my closet were *that* big, maybe you and Noah wouldn't have found me when I was hiding out."

"We would have found you," she said. "We could smell you the moment we walked in. All we had to do was follow our noses. They led us straight to where you were hiding."

The moment they'd decided to come to my apartment, I hadn't stood a chance.

"I'm sorry I stabbed you," I said. "I was just so terrified when I was in there. I had no idea who was breaking in, so when you opened the door to the closet, I just... reacted."

"No need to apologize," she said. "I would have done the same thing in your shoes. Speaking of..." She dug through piles upon piles of shoes in her closet, eventually holding up a worn pair of black combat boots. "Can you fit into size eights?"

"I'm a seven and a half, but it should be fine," I said.

"Good." She tossed the shoes over at me, one after the other. They landed right in front of my feet. "Try those on."

I did as asked. They were *slightly* too big, but they'd work. They were also a total different style than anything I'd ever worn. The boots I owned were all shiny and sleek, whereas these laced up all the way to the top. They made me look like *way* more of a badass than I'd ever felt I had the potential to be.

"What's this for?" I asked, poking a strange, narrow pocket on the inner side of one of the boots.

"For this." She walked over to her lingerie chest, opened the top drawer, and pulled out a shiny knife. "You got a good stab at me with that crystal wand, but I figured this would be a more practical way to defend yourself in the future."

I took the knife from her and studied it. It felt

awkward and uncomfortable to hold. I'd always been the non-violent type—I supposed non-violence was bound to rub off on me from living with my mom.

But I was smart enough to know that while accompanying two shifters on a hunt to kill demons, I needed a way to defend myself. There wouldn't always be crystal wands—or other everyday objects that could double as weapons—nearby for the taking.

"You put it in the pocket of your left boot," Sage said. "That is, assuming you're right handed?"

"I am." I reached down and placed the knife in the pocket. It fit snugly inside, and I took a few practice steps to see how it felt.

It would take a bit of time to get used to one shoe weighing more than the other, but I hoped I'd adjust quickly.

"And Sage?" I asked, and she turned back around to look at me. "Thank you. Everything that you—and Noah —are doing to help me find my mom means a lot. I don't know how I'll ever be able to repay you…"

"If you pass the Angel Trials, I'm sure we'll figure *something* out," she said with a wink.

"What exactly *are* the Angel Trials?" I asked, since no one had given me a direct explanation yet.

"I'm not sure." She ran a hand through her hair, as if the question made her nervous. "All I know is that it's a way for the Earth Angel to decide which humans to turn into Nephilim."

"It's going to be dangerous," I said. "Isn't it?"

"Probably." Her eyes were serious, but she shook it off, replacing the seriousness with a smile. "But I doubt it'll be any more dangerous than coming with me and Noah on our demon hunt. And there's no point in worrying about it yet. Let's just focus on the task at hand—finding you some clothes that fit so you're not stuck wearing the same smelly outfit for our entire journey."

RAVEN

IT DIDN'T TAKE LONG to find and pack up some jeans and tanks that fit me. Sage also had some never-been-worn underwear with the tags still on, which would last long enough until we could stop by a store to pick up a pack of my own.

"I think that's it," Sage said, zipping up the packed bag.

"How are we going to fit the bags *and* ourselves on the motorcycles?" I asked.

"We won't be taking the bikes," she said. "It'll be too difficult with you tagging along."

I frowned at the reminder of how much of an inconvenience I was to them. "Without the bikes, how are we getting to New Orleans?" I asked. "I'm guessing we can't fly, since there's no way we'd be able to get all the weapons through security."

"We'd have to fly private to avoid security," she said. "I asked Flint for permission to take the jet, but he said no. My insufferable brother refuses to make this easy for us. So we'll be taking my car, Margo."

"You named your car?" I raised an eyebrow.

"Cars are part of the family." She crossed her arms, looking truly offended. "Every car needs a good name."

"Well, I'm looking forward to meeting Margo," I said. "And I'm not gonna lie—I'm glad we're going by car. My hair's barely survived a few motorcycle rides through LA—I doubt it would make it on a drive halfway across the country."

"I'm with you on that," she said, running her fingers through her own long hair. "But Noah *hates* cars. He says they're too confining. He's why we got the bikes in the first place."

"Speaking of Noah," I started, figuring that now—before we left on the journey—was my time to bring this up without making anything awkward. "Are the two of you together? Like, are you dating?" My voice rose too much at the end of each question, and I felt my cheeks heat up again in the clear indication that they were turning bright pink.

My attempt at not being awkward had clearly failed drastically.

"Why are you asking?" She tilted her head, a knowing smile on her face.

"No reason," I said quickly.

"Really?" She raised an eyebrow. "Don't you think that if Noah and I were dating, I would have been pissed about what I walked in on earlier?" She pointed her thumb toward the pool house, although it wasn't necessary since I knew what she was referring to.

"We weren't doing anything," I said. "We were just talking."

"You were staring at each other like you couldn't wait to rip each other's clothes off." She held up a hand to stop me from speaking. "Don't deny it—I'm not blind."

I pressed my lips together, knowing that denying it would be futile. But I didn't want to admit to it, either.

"You're not mad?" I said instead.

"Noah and I are hunting partners," she said. "We're definitely not dating. It's not like that between us, and it's not ever *going* to be like that between us. You can trust me on that."

"How can you be so sure?" I asked. "You're both single, you're both attractive, and you've been doing a lot of traveling together while hunting…" I let the final part hang, since it was more than obvious where I was going with this. "You're both being extremely generous by helping me find my mom, so if you have any feelings for him, I don't want to impose. That's all. Not like I think he's even interested in me—because I don't think he is—but I thought it would be best to be up front with each other."

Sage shook her head and gave me a close-lipped smile, as if everything I'd just said amused her. "In the conversation you were having with Noah about shifters, I guess he didn't get to the part about imprinting and mating, did he?" she asked.

"No…" I said, my eyes wide. I'd never heard of the word "imprinting" before, but I knew enough about mating to have an idea about where this conversation might be heading.

Sage jumped onto her bed, situating herself amongst the massive amounts of shiny, glittery pillows. "Come, sit," she said with a smile, motioning to the end of the bed. "You'll want to make yourself comfortable for this one."

I wasn't sure what had spurned this sudden girlish comfort she apparently felt around me, but I did as she asked, perching on the end of the bed.

"Do you believe in soul mates?" she asked.

Apparently, we were jumping straight into the deep stuff.

"I don't know." I shrugged, since it was a complicated question. "I've always thought it was unlikely that there's only *one* person out there for each person. With billions of people in the world, the chances of meeting your soul mate would be slim to none. Those odds are incredibly depressing."

"Unless there was a divine plan that made sure you'd run into your soul mate when you were ready to meet them," she suggested.

"Maybe." It was the type of fairy tale idea I'd have scoffed at before, but after being exposed to the supernatural world, I had no idea what to believe anymore. "I guess I've always looked at it like this—there are some people who we're naturally more attracted to and drawn to than others. If both people feel that connection and choose to act on it, they can fall in love and become soul mates. So, a person has a bunch of possible soul mates out there, and eventually chooses the one they want to spend the rest of their life with."

"Interesting." She studied me, nodding slowly. "What you just described is similar to the shifter process of imprinting and mating."

RAVEN

"CARE TO EXPLAIN?" I had a feeling she was going to anyway, but I might as well push her along.

"Shifters can imprint on multiple people," she said. "It happens after sharing their first kiss, and it's always felt mutually."

"What does it feel like?" I asked.

"I don't know." Sage shrugged. "I've never imprinted on anyone."

"Really?" I didn't hide my shock. "Is that typical?"

"No." She pulled her legs inward, so she was sitting curled up in a ball. "Most shifters my age have imprinted on a few others by now. No one knows why I haven't. When I was a little younger than you, I swear I must have kissed every shifter in the state on a quest to find *someone* to imprint on. But nope—it never happened."

"I'm sorry," I said. "That must be frustrating."

"It is what it is." She forced a smile, although I could tell it bothered her. "New shifters don't move to town often—we usually stay with our packs. So when Noah came to LA, I thought *maybe* we'd imprint on each other. I tried, but nope. No imprint."

"So you kissed?" I immediately pictured it in my mind, and jealously surged through my chest. But I pushed it away. Because she'd confirmed they weren't imprinted.

So why did just the *thought* of them kissing make me feel jealous anyway?

"We did," she said. "But don't look so distraught about it. Neither of us felt anything. It was like kissing a sibling." She shuddered. "It was weird, and trust me, we haven't kissed since. We both like to pretend it never happened."

I didn't realize I'd looked distraught, so I tried to rearrange my features to appear more neutral. I was always terrible at keeping my emotions from my face.

"Anyway," she said. "Imprinting is supposedly pretty intense. Most shifters mate with the first person they imprint on, although it's not always the case. We're encouraged to wait until we're at least eighteen to seal the bond. We have a saying—imprint by nature, mate by choice."

"Mating is the equivalent to marriage?" I asked.

"It's a *much* stronger bond," she said. "Mating connects our minds, bodies, and souls. And shifters only mate once. So once we mate, that's it. We'll never imprint or mate with anyone else again for the rest of our lives."

"Never?" I couldn't keep the shock from my voice, because while it was romantic, it was also extreme. "Not even if one of them dies?"

"Not even then," she said. "The widowed are highly respected in the packs, mainly because we all feel terribly for those who have lost their mates and will never love again until reuniting in the Beyond."

We were both silent for a few seconds, and I took in the incredible commitment it took to make such a bond.

It would take two people who truly loved each other —a love stronger than anything else in the world. I'd always hoped that someday I'd experience a love that strong.

"Is that why it seemed like Noah was trying to kiss me back in the pool house?" I asked, trying to lighten the mood. "Was he trying to see if we imprinted on each other?"

"No way." She sat back, shocked.

"Why's that so crazy?" I asked, although the moment the words were out of my mouth, a possibility hit me.

"He's not widowed, right? Is that why he left his pack? Because he lost his mate?"

"No!" She stopped me from talking before I could continue. "Noah's never mated with anyone."

"So why'd you react like that?"

"Because shifters can only imprint on other shifters," she said. "We've never imprinted outside of our species —not even on other supernaturals."

"Oh." I deflated, feeling like I'd just been punched in the gut. "So he was just toying with me back there?"

I'd suspected as much, but it was a whole different thing to have my suspicions confirmed. And it hurt way more than I'd expected.

"I wouldn't say he was *toying* with you." Her expression softened, and she twirled a strand of hair around her finger. "Noah's been through a lot, but he's a good guy. He would never purposefully hurt you."

"Hm," I said, since he was *definitely* flirting with me back in the pool house. "Well, I'm not into casual hook ups." I sat straighter, trying to maintain what little dignity I felt like I had left. "So I'm glad you told me all of this, so I know to keep my guard up."

"Yeah," she agreed. "I mean, I honestly do think he likes you. But no matter how attracted to you he is now, he'll eventually imprint and mate with another shifter. Once that happens, he'll be devoted to her completely.

Any romantic feelings he had for anyone else in the past will be inconsequential in comparison for the love he'll feel for his mate. You can't let yourself forget that."

"Right." I tried to sound stoic, although I hated how my heart hurt now that the possibility of anything real developing between Noah and me had been crushed. "I wish he'd been upfront with me about all of this *before* getting all flirty, but what's done is done. At least now I can let him know where I stand and we can focus on what's important—hunting demons and getting to Avalon."

38

RAVEN

SAGE and I chatted for a bit longer. Well, mainly she listened as I vented about how worried I was for my mom and how scared I was for everything coming next.

She did her best to assure me that it would all turn out fine, but I knew the promises were empty. None of us knew how any of this would turn out. All we could do was try our best and hope it was enough.

I changed into another pair of Sage's pajamas—this time, into a pair that fit me much better—and headed back to the pool house. I was getting ready to knock when the door opened. Noah must have heard me approaching.

His hair was wet, and he was only wearing a towel tied around his waist—he'd apparently just gotten out of the shower. My cheeks flushed as I gaped at his perfectly defined body, unable to keep myself from checking him out.

"Like what you see?" He smirked and leaned against the doorframe.

Did he even have to ask? I was sure my expression was answer enough.

But I needed to get control of myself. It was difficult when he was tempting me so much, but this just reminded me that I had to be upfront with him about where I stood sooner rather than later.

"Save it." I rolled my eyes, forcing my way past him. I couldn't even look at him, not trusting myself to resist checking him out again until he put some clothes on.

"Whoa." He shut the door behind him, sounding genuinely surprised. "Why the sudden ice princess attitude?"

I spun around to face him, making sure to breathe steadily and stay in control. I couldn't let him see how much he was affecting me. "Sage told me about the imprinting and mating thing that shifters do," I said. "Since I'm a human and nothing serious can ever happen between us, I'd like for whatever flirtation that's going on between us to end here. So if you could put on some clothes, that would be great."

His eyes dimmed. If I didn't know any better, I'd think he was let down.

But he just walked back to his room, presumably to respect my wishes and get dressed.

I curled up on the big armchair, disappointment crushing my chest. The feeling made no sense. I should have been glad that Noah was respecting my wishes—not disappointed.

He came back out less than a minute later dressed in pajamas nearly identical to the ones he wore last night. With his wet hair pressed to his forehead, he looked younger and more vulnerable than ever. "I'm sorry." He stared down at me, looking like he genuinely meant it. "I planned on telling you."

"When?" I reached for the lapis crystal on my neck, as if it could give me strength. "Because before Sage interrupted us earlier, you seemed a lot closer to kissing me than to telling me."

His eyes hardened, and I felt more of a wall between us than ever before. "It won't happen again," he said. "I promise."

"Good." I wished I felt as content with his response as I sounded.

Silence descended upon us. I couldn't help wondering if he'd ever imprinted before, and if so, why he hadn't mated with her. But it was a deeply personal question, so I stopped myself from asking. Instead, I continued playing with the crystal, wishing I could figure out something else to say to break the tension.

I couldn't shut up before, but now that I *needed* to speak? I was coming up with nothing.

"You shouldn't wear your mom's necklace while we're demon hunting," he said suddenly.

"Why not?" I whipped up my head to look at him, gripping the crystal protectively.

"Because the demons want it."

"They didn't want the necklace," I said. "They wanted my mom. Otherwise, why would Azazel have left it at the witches' mansion?"

"Hm." He paused. "Good point."

"Did you just admit I was right?" I raised an eyebrow, unable to keep from smiling.

"I said you made a good point," he repeated.

"Meaning I was right."

"Perhaps." Amusement flickered in his eyes.

Heat rose in my stomach at the way he was looking at me. It was similar to the way he'd looked at me earlier, when he'd corrected me about the difference between werewolves and shifters. Earlier... when he'd pressed me against the wall and had been about to kiss me.

But I needed to squelch the feeling immediately.

Because no matter how Noah was looking at me now, it was irrelevant.

If I fell for him, I'd end up heartbroken once he imprinted and mated with someone else.

"Anyway," I continued in as business-like of a manner as possible, determined to break whatever connection had just flared between us. "If the demons wanted the necklace, wouldn't that be a reason for us to keep the necklace *with* us? We could use it to bait them."

"It would be." Pride shined in his eyes. "Maybe you won't be so bad at demon hunting after all."

"Maybe not." My heart thudded in my chest, and I couldn't look away from him. Every inch of my body wanted to resume what had started between us earlier.

But I couldn't give into temptation. My life was already falling apart enough as it was. I refused to add heartbreak to my growing list of problems.

"It's getting late." I stood, and my eyes darted around the room, trying desperately to look anywhere but at Noah. "I should go to bed. Like you said, it's important to get as much sleep as possible when we have time to grab it…" I was babbling now, so I placed my hands on the back of the chair and gave him a single nod. "Goodnight."

"This early?" He sounded surprised. "I thought for

sure that your inquisition about the supernatural world was only just getting started."

"We've got a long road trip ahead of us," I said. "Don't worry—I'll come prepared with questions."

"You better." Challenge glinted in his gaze.

I hurried into his room, not breathing until I'd closed the door behind me. Then I leaned back against it, frustration mounting in my veins. Because he was right—I *did* have a lot of questions.

I just didn't trust myself to stay in the room with him looking at me like that and remain *focused* on those questions.

Plus, on the road trip I'd be in the car with both him *and* Sage. It would be better that way. Because the less time I spent alone with Noah, the less likely I'd be to fall for him.

Then once we got to Avalon, we could go our separate ways and never have to see each other again.

39

RAVEN

SAGE'S CAR—MARGO—WAS a shiny white Range Rover. It had by far enough room for us to pack up all of our stuff for the trip, along with the weapons and potions that Sage and Noah brought. They had an entire bag full of potions, the vials inside different sizes and full of a variety of colored liquids. Some of the potions were even in little pods, like laundry detergent. They looked perfect for throwing.

"What're all the potions for?" I asked as Noah placed the bag on the floor of the backseat. I assumed he put it there so the contents inside wouldn't break.

"Truth potions, memory potions, invisibility potions... we've got a bit of everything we might need," he said. "That's another rule of demon hunting—always be prepared for anything."

"Memory potions?" I blinked, not liking the sound of that. It made my brain itch, and I scratched at my forehead, although it did nothing to help. "What do those do?"

"They can erase and replace a person's memory." Sage grinned. "Most of the time humans will come up with logical explanations for the supernatural, so we don't have to worry about erasing their memories if they see something they shouldn't. But if they don't, memory potion can come in handy."

I froze in place, not liking the sound of that. "How much does it erase?" I asked.

"It can erase and replace a day or two, maybe a few days, tops," she said. "Like any potion, it's much more potent if it's injected or ingested than thrown, but the pods will do the trick if we only need to erase a bit."

"Is it possible to erase more than that?" I wasn't sure why I was so interested, but I was. Something inside of me—something I didn't recognize—compelled me to ask. "Can it erase weeks?"

"Not any that I've seen on the market," she said. "That would take more magic than even Amber and her circle could do. Plus, a potion like that would be beyond expensive."

"But it exists?"

"I don't know," she said. "Maybe."

"Why so many questions about the memory potion?" Noah asked.

"I don't know." I shrugged. The answer felt like it was on the tip of my tongue, but it disappeared a second later. "Something about it makes me feel... eerie. It's hard to explain. I just don't like the sound of it."

"If you're worried we'll use it on you, don't be." His eyes turned serious. "You're part of our team now. You can trust us."

Sage watched us with a knowing smirk and twirled the keys around her fingers, hopping into the driver's seat.

"I know I can," I said it instinctively, since it was true —I *did* trust them. "I was just curious. And you told me to bring questions, didn't you?" I added a bit of teasing into my tone, not liking that he'd even considered that I might not trust them.

I didn't trust easily, but after everything they'd done for me, they'd earned my trust and more.

"That I did," he said. "I just didn't realize the inquisition would start before even leaving the compound." He walked to the passenger side and opened the door, motioning for me to get in. "Now, are you coming or what?"

"You're letting me sit in the front?" I balked, especially when he nodded in confirmation. "No way. Your legs are longer than mine. I'm fine in the back. You take the front."

"I'm terrible at navigating," he said. "Sage will be relieved to have you as a co-pilot."

"It's true," Sage piped in. "Get in the front. As the driver, I insist."

"If you both say so." I felt bad taking the front away from Noah, but they were being so pushy about it that it seemed silly to argue further.

Once Noah and I were situated in our seats, Sage pulled out of the compound. She stopped the moment we were past the gates.

"Why'd you stop?" I asked. "Did you forget something?"

"No," she said. "It's just time for you to give me my ring back."

"Oh, right." I pulled the black tourmaline ring off my finger and handed it to her. "Why'd I need to wear it there, anyway? It's not like your pack didn't know I was there."

She placed the ring back on her finger, purposefully not looking at me as she pressed down on the gas and drove us away from the compound.

"Guys?" I twisted around to face Noah, hoping *he'd* answer my question. "What are you not telling me?"

Darkness crept over Noah's eyes. He turned away to

look out the window, his brow crinkled as if he couldn't face my question.

"Why did I have to wear a ring that concealed my scent at the compound?" I repeated, glancing back and forth between Noah and Sage. "Do shifters have a... problem with humans?"

"Not a problem, exactly." Noah finally turned to face me again, his expression full of resolve. "But there's one big question you haven't asked yet that's pretty important."

"There are a *lot* of questions I haven't asked yet that are important," I said. "But which one did you have in mind?"

"The most important one in regards to a predator." He tilted his head, his eyes taking on a hungry glint as he gazed at me. "The question about our diet."

40

RAVEN

"I've shared a few meals with you by now," I said. "I've seen what you eat. You eat meat. A *lot* of meat."

"Yes," Noah said. "And what, exactly, do you think you are?"

"I'm a human," I said. But then I froze in place, my eyes widening in horror as the possibility of what he was saying dawned on me. "You're not saying... you don't eat *humans*. Do you?"

"Those of us in control of our humanity don't," he said. "But do you remember what I told you yesterday, about how we only shift when necessary to make sure we maintain control over our humanity?"

"Of course," I said.

"Well, some of us have better control over our humanity than others."

I should have been scared. After all, I was in a car with two wolf shifters, one who had just admitted that some of them struggle with control over their humanity and that they *eat people*.

But I wasn't scared. Because I trusted that Noah and Sage were good. They had my back. I believed them that not *all* shifters were good, but I knew in my gut that they would never hurt me.

"Okay." I kept my voice steady, wanting him to know that despite what he was saying, I trusted them. "So since I had to wear the ring to cover my scent in the compound, I'm going to guess that not all the shifters in the Montgomery pack are in full control of their humanity?"

"Bingo," Sage said. "I'm sure you noticed that my brother Flint is the alpha of the pack, right?"

"I could tell he was the leader," I said. "Is he the one who... struggles with his humanity?" I initially wanted to ask if he was the one who *ate people*, but I held myself back. The idea was too gruesome to say out loud.

"As the alpha, his wolf side is strong," Noah said. "Like most shifters who live in civilization, he has it under control for the most part. He wouldn't be able to live in the city if he didn't."

"His trouble is in his sleep," Sage continued. "If he'd smelled your fresh human scent in his sleep, his animal

side might have risen while he was unconscious, and..."
She trailed off, letting me come to my own conclusion.
That he would have attacked me. "The ring kept you
safe," she said. "That's what matters."

"Right." I nodded—it was a lot to take in. But even
though I trusted them, I had to ask my next question for
my own protection. "I don't have anything to worry
about when you both are sleeping, do I?"

"No," Noah said quickly. "That's a problem unique to
alphas, since their animal sides are so strong."

"I'm surprised you're not an alpha." The words came
out of my mouth before I realized what I was saying. "I
just mean that you seem like such a take charge type of
guy."

"I already told you." He leaned back, his eyes going
distant. "I'm a lone wolf."

"Of course." I wanted to ask more. But it was clear
that mentions of his past made Noah shut down, so I
focused on other questions as we drove out of LA and
into the desert.

I had a *lot* of other questions, and as we started off
our drive to New Orleans, I learned a lot about the
supernatural world and the creatures within it.

The first thing I learned was that the three main
types of supernaturals in the world were shifters,
witches, and vampires.

Shifters weren't immortal—they had the same lifespans as humans. They were numerous and lived in packs all over the world. The animal they could shift into was the strongest predator of the region they lived in. Some packs had integrated with society and remained mainly in their human forms. Others lived in the wilderness, their animal sides having taken over completely. Those were the dangerous ones—the ones who would eat any prey they came across, including humans.

Vampires lived mainly in one of their six designated kingdoms—one kingdom in each continent. The kingdoms were all different, but each one was extremely powerful. From what Noah and Sage said, most vampires were pretty pompous and interacted with the rest of society as infrequently as possible. There were a few rogue vampire covens living amongst humans, but not many.

Strong witches were rare. The strongest of them lived in the vampire kingdoms, like royalty. Others, like Amber and her circle, lived in society and charged hefty fees for their services. But most witches weren't strong, and were only capable of small party tricks. Those witches had pretty much integrated with human society completely at this point.

"Do you think that's what my mom could be?" I asked. "A weak witch?"

"No." Noah sounded absolutely sure of it. "Even the weakest witches still smell like witch. And as her daughter, you would have inherited her magic no matter what."

"What about the Nephilim?" I asked.

"What about them?" he asked in return.

"So far you've told me about shifters, vampires, and witches," I said. "But there are also Nephilim. Rosella mentioned them herself. Where do they fit in with all of this?"

"The Nephilim are an extinct race," Sage said. "Well, almost extinct. Annika—the Earth Angel—was the last one left."

"But Nephilim are the only ones who can kill greater demons," I recalled what Amber had said back at her mansion.

"They are," Noah said. "Which is why Annika is creating a new army of Nephilim."

"By having humans go through the Angel Trials?"

"Yep," he confirmed. "When Annika was turned into the Earth Angel, she was given the Holy Grail."

"*The* Holy Grail?" I interrupted, shocked.

"Yes." He laughed. "*The* Holy Grail. It has the power to turn humans into Nephilim."

"Which is why I'm going to Avalon." My stomach felt hollow with the intensity of it all. "To go through the Angel Trials and become a Nephilim." The thought terrified me. But if I let myself think about it too much, I'd go nuts. So I needed to know more. "What exactly *are* the Angel Trials?" I asked, hoping Noah would at least know *something*. "I want to be as prepared as possible so I'm able to get through them."

"I don't know," Noah said. "I've never been to Avalon."

"And I already told you that I don't know," Sage said. "I've never even met the Earth Angel. Everything I know about her is through Noah."

"How *do* you know her?" I twisted back around to face Noah.

"It's a long story." He ran his hand through his hair and gazed out the window. From the far off look in his eyes, it was clear he didn't want to share that story.

"We're road tripping from LA to New Orleans," I said. "I think we have enough time for a long story or two."

"I barely know her." He returned his gaze to mine, as if that answer should be good enough. "I only met her once—when she gave me the task of killing ten demons for entrance to Avalon."

"That wasn't a long story," I said. "It was two sentences."

He shrugged, saying nothing.

He was hiding something from me, and I was determined to find out what that something was. But I also knew not to push it. We had a long journey ahead, which meant a lot of time to build trust. He'd tell me when he was ready.

In the meantime, I was getting the vibe that it was time to change subjects.

"So, shifters can only imprint on shifters," I started, noticing how Noah noticeably stiffened the moment I said the word "imprint."

"Yep." He sounded bored. He was also purposefully not looking at me.

"But like you said before, there are various types of shifters—wolves, coyotes, lions, bears," I said. "Can wolf shifters only imprint on other wolf shifters? Or can they imprint on the other types too?"

Sage glanced back at Noah. She'd been letting him do most of the talking so far, but she must have picked up from his body language that he didn't want to discuss it, because she was the one who answered me.

"We usually imprint on shifters who share the same animal nature that we do," she said. "But not always."

"What happens then?" I asked.

"Like I said, it's rare," she said. "It only happens to a handful of shifters each generation, if ever. But when shifters choose a mate, the two of their minds, bodies, and souls become connected. This process changes both people—and it allows those rare shifters to both be able to shift into both their natural animal and their mate's natural animal. They're called dyads. There aren't many dyads, but those that exist are revered amongst our kind."

"Wow," I said. "So if a wolf shifter and a bear shifter mated, both of them would be able to shift into both a wolf *and* a bear?"

"Yes," she said.

"And what about their kids?" I asked. "Would they be able to shift into both animals too?"

"Nope," she said. "When we mate, the couple joins the pack belonging to the more dominant of the two. So if the wolf and bear joined the wolf's pack, their kids would only be able to shift into wolves, and vice versa."

"Interesting," I said.

"Not really." Noah finally decided to speak again. "And not relevant to you."

"Someone's touchy," I muttered.

"Don't mind him," Sage said. "He doesn't like being in cars—he says they make him feel closed in. That's why we got the motorcycles."

"All right." I was starting to wish I hadn't brought up imprinting and mating again in the first place. "So, why don't you tell me more about those potions you brought with us? If I'm going to be helping you kill demons, I might as well know what we're working with."

"You're not helping us kill demons," Noah said. "You're standing back and staying safe while *Sage and I* kill demons. Big difference."

"I can help." I crossed my arms and glared at him. "I'm not useless, you know."

"You're human," he said. "Compared to supernaturals, you're pretty useless in a fight."

I took a sharp breath inward, his words stinging. Is that what he really thought of me? That I was *useless*?

That was a load of bullshit.

"I'm not useless." I turned back around, refusing to look back at him again.

At least Sage didn't think I was useless. She wouldn't have given me that knife if she did.

"You said some of those potions were in pods that you could throw," I said to her. "I can use them if I know what's in them."

"First of all, you should know that potions are defensive, not offensive," she said. "They can help in a fight, but they won't do any fighting for you. Still, there's no reason why you can't learn about them."

I smiled back at Noah in victory.

He just looked out the window, pretending that both of us weren't there.

Fine by me. I had better things to do—like listen to Sage as she taught me about the different potions and how to use them.

There was no time like the present to prepare for a demon hunting journey.

41

RAVEN

IT WAS A TWENTY-NINE HOUR DRIVE, straight east on the 10 to get from LA to New Orleans. The majority of the trip so far had been through deserts. I'd known the country was big, but I never realized how much open, empty land there was until driving through it. It seemed like the desert went on forever and ever, with no end in sight.

Since we couldn't afford to lose any time by stopping for the night to sleep, we drove in shifts. Well, Noah and Sage drove in shifts. Neither of them let me take the wheel, despite my offers.

Apparently, they thought humans were useless at driving, too.

Once Noah took the wheel, Sage fell asleep pretty

soon after hopping into the back. Without her constant chatter, awkward silence settled between Noah and I.

I tried to ask a few more questions about the supernatural world, but he kept giving me short, single word answers. He clearly didn't feel like talking anymore.

Soon after the sun set, my eyes started to droop, so I gave in and fell asleep.

I woke up as Noah was pulling off the freeway toward a gas station. A quick glance behind me showed that Sage was still sleeping in the back. She looked mighty comfortable under the blanket she'd retrieved from the trunk.

"Where are we?" I said quietly to Noah, not wanting to wake Sage.

"Dunno." He shrugged. "Somewhere in the desert."

"That's helpful." I rolled my eyes. "Did we cross into New Mexico yet?" We'd just passed Tucson, Arizona—where we'd stopped for dinner—when I'd fallen asleep. A glance at the clock on the dashboard showed that I'd slept for four hours, so I figured we must have crossed the state border by now.

"Check for yourself." He motioned to the phone, which was plugged in as it tracked our route. "Unless that's too difficult a task for you?"

Someone was touchy. And I didn't feel a need to

garner his rudeness with a response. So I checked the GPS on the phone and saw that yes, we'd crossed into New Mexico a while ago and were currently nearing the Texas border.

"If you want to take a break, I can drive for a bit," I offered once he'd pulled up to the pump.

Judging by how cranky he was, he was in desperate need of a nap.

"I'm good for another few hours, and then Sage will be up to take over." He reached into his pants pocket and pulled out a credit card. "But if you want to help, you can pump the gas."

"Seriously?" I crossed my arms and glanced down at the card, not taking it. "You won't let me drive, but you want me to pump the gas?"

"You were the one who said you weren't useless..." he trailed.

Anger simmered in my veins. Of course I wasn't useless. But not letting me drive and then asking me to pump the gas felt so *degrading*. Like I was some kind of servant.

I wanted to say that no, he could pump his own gas.

But if I didn't pump the gas, I was *definitely* being useless.

It was a lose-lose situation.

"Fine." I snatched the credit card from his hand, flipped my hair over my shoulder, and stomped out of the car to pump the gas. As the tank filled, I heard a howl in the distance—a coyote? Whatever it was made the hairs rise on my arms.

Once the nozzle clicked that it was done, I got back in the passenger seat and handed the card back to Noah, not saying a word.

He started up the car, nodding when the needle pointed to full.

"Did I do a good enough job of filling the tank up for you?" I didn't bother keeping the sarcasm from my tone.

"Fantastic." He pulled out of the station, stopped at the intersection, and looked to me for guidance. "Which way do I go?" he asked.

"You go east on the 10…" I trailed. "The same way we've been going for this entire drive."

"I know that." His jaw tightened, his knuckles turning white as they held the steering wheel. "Just tell me which way to turn."

I looked ahead at the two signs that *clearly* stated which freeway entrance led east and which led west. "Follow the sign that says east." I casually motioned to the signs ahead of us. "Unless that's too difficult a task for you?" I smirked in amusement. Throwing his own words back in his face might have been childish, but it was so, so sweet.

"Just tell me which way to turn." His tone was clipped, and from the way he was glaring at me, I feared he might whip out his claws at any moment.

"Do you have a vision problem?" I asked, suddenly worried that I was a passenger in a car with a driver who needed glasses. "Can you not see the signs?"

"I don't have a vision problem," he said. "Shifters have enhanced senses. My vision is far superior than that of a human."

What he *really* meant was clear—that his vision was far superior to mine.

"Yet you can't see the signs right in front of us." I narrowed my eyes at him, suddenly suspicious that he wasn't being honest with me. But he'd shown no signs of vision issues in the past.

So what could he possibly have to lie about right now? Why was he commanding me to give him directions?

As I studied him, the pieces started to come together.

Sage had said he was the world's worst co-pilot. He'd refused to check the map on the phone. He'd all but forced me to pump the gas for him. Now he didn't know which sign was east and which was west.

"You can't read," I voiced my suspicion out loud.

"You can *see* the signs, but you don't know which way to turn because you don't know how to *read* them."

The way he straightened and gripped the wheel tighter, all while refusing to look at me, confirmed my suspicion.

I sat back, baffled. I'd never met someone who was illiterate. What kind of life had he grown up in where he hadn't been taught how to read?

Up until now, his refusal to open up about his past had annoyed me. But with this revelation, my heart went out to him.

"Left," I said softly. "You take the entrance on the left."

He did as I said, turning up the radio as he entered the freeway. Sage stirred but didn't wake. We were in the middle of nowhere, and there were no other cars on the road but ours.

It didn't take long for the questions to build up so much inside of me that I felt like I was going to explode if I didn't say something.

"You're not from around here, are you?" I finally asked.

"Here?" He laughed. "No. Wolves don't live in deserts. At least, not *my* species of wolf."

"That's not what I meant," I said, since of course I

knew he wasn't from *the desert*. "I meant from California. LA. Well, from a city in general."

"You want to know why I can't read."

"Yes," I said, but then I pressed my lips together, realizing that might sound harsher than intended. "Well, I'm curious about where you're from where they didn't teach you how to read."

He was silent for a few seconds, as if debating what to tell me.

I *so* badly wanted to ask more questions—to lead him on a process of elimination to figure out what state he was from—but I held my tongue.

One big thing I'd learned about Noah was that he held his cards until he was ready to show them. So I waited, tugging at the ends of my sleeves as the question lingered between us.

"You're right," he finally said.

"About what?" That wasn't the answer I'd expected, but I was intrigued nonetheless.

"That I could use some rest," he said, and I deflated at the realization that he wasn't about to share details about his past. "Do you want a turn at the wheel?"

I wanted to say no—that he could keep driving if that meant we could keep talking.

But then I remembered the Chariot card I'd drawn from the tarot deck.

Get behind the wheel and be the driver of your own destiny.

"Sure," I replied instead.

After all, what better way to be the Charioteer of the journey than by driving Sage Montgomery's Range Rover?

42

RAVEN

I'D CROSSED the border into west Texas what felt like ages ago, although a glance at the dashboard clock showed that only two hours had passed.

It was past midnight, and I was the only car on the road this far out in the middle of nowhere. It was also incredibly dark. Even the freeway didn't have lights out here. Both Sage and Noah were fast asleep—Sage still in the back, and Noah in the passenger seat—which meant I had only the radio and my own thoughts to keep me company. Luckily, the Range Rover had satellite radio. I doubted any regular stations broadcasted this far out.

If someone had told me a few days ago about everything that was going to happen to me since my twenty-first birthday, I never would have believed it. I would have thought they were crazy.

Now here I was, driving a car full of weapons and potions with two wolf shifters as passengers, on a quest to hunt and kill four demons for admittance to a magical island where I'd compete in trials that would eventually lead to saving my mom from the greater demon who'd abducted her.

There was so much to think about and worry about. How would I prove that I wasn't useless on the demon hunting mission? What would I be facing in the angel trials? Where had Azazel taken my mom, and what did he want with her? Was she safe? Was she hungry? Was she scared?

At the thought of my mom's abduction, a memory slammed into my mind—it was from the nightmare I'd had the other night. In the dream, I'd been captured. I'd been gripping onto jail bars, screaming for help. There had been two others in there with me, and I'd seen our kidnapper, too. She was a young woman who looked like a flapper.

What if that hadn't been a dream? What if I'd somehow connected to my mom's mind and was witnessing her actual experience?

Logically, it was more likely that just *knowing* my mom had been abducted had made me have a nightmare about being abducted myself. But I had to hold on to hope that maybe—just *maybe*—it was a clue about where she was.

Without hope, what did I have left?

Once Sage and Noah woke up, I'd ask them their thoughts. So many things I'd previously thought were impossible were real, so why should this be any different?

Suddenly, headlights shined from behind me. The car quickly gained traction. The driver was going exceptionally fast—they must have figured they wouldn't get pulled over for speeding this far out in the middle of nowhere—so I moved over to the right lane to let them pass.

But it wasn't just one car. It was three. No—*four* of them. A group caravan, I supposed.

The first one passed me, like I assumed it would. It was a pickup truck. I couldn't see it well because it was dark, but it looked old.

I stared straight ahead—I didn't like to look into other cars as I drove. You never knew if the people inside would be creepers and make vulgar gestures. I'd always found it was best to be safe and ignore them completely.

Instead of continuing along the fast lane, the truck swerved into the right lane, right in front of me.

I screamed an obscenity, moving my foot over to the

brake just in time to slow down and avoid crashing into them.

Sage and Noah jolted awake.

"What's going on?" Noah's eyes were full of alarm.

"That truck just cut me off!" I glared at the truck ahead of me. "But no worries—I braked in time."

A second later, I worried I'd spoken too soon. Because one of the other trucks lined up parallel with me in the left lane. Another trailed behind me. The fourth pulled to the right, driving next to me in the emergency lane.

They had us surrounded. And now that our headlights were brightening the area, I saw that each truck had gleaming spikes jutting out from the centers of its tires.

I cursed again and gripped the steering wheel, fear numbing my veins. I was a decent driver—I could handle LA traffic like a pro—but being cornered and chased in the middle of the West Texas desert was a completely different ballgame.

One I'd certainly never expected to be playing.

"Who are they?" I asked, panicked now. "Why are they doing this? Are they demons?"

"Relax." Noah's voice was calm—*too* calm. "Stay in your lane, and don't get too close to any of their trucks."

I did as he said, finally glancing aside to see who was in the truck next to me.

Two grungy men with long, greasy hair leered at me. I snapped my eyes away from theirs, regretting looking over in the first place.

Meanwhile, Sage opened one of the back windows and took a deep breath. "They're shifters," she said as she closed up the window. "Coyote shifters, from the smell of them."

"What do they want with us?" I asked.

"No idea." She moved around and held something out in the console between Noah and me. "But you should wear this."

I glanced to the side to see what she was talking about.

It was her black tourmaline ring—the one with the cloaking spell.

"Why?" I asked, although the answer came to me a second later, bringing the leering gazes to an entirely new level. "You don't think they want to *eat me*... do you?"

I knew there weren't many places to buy food out here in the middle of nowhere, but this seemed like an extreme measure for *anyone* to go to for a bite to eat— even a pack of wild coyote shifters.

"It's possible." Noah took the ring from Sage and

held it out to me. "We have no idea how civilized these shifters are."

"And because our rings hide my and Noah's scents, the coyotes probably assume we're all humans," Sage added. "Which is why they're cornering us like prey. Once they know we're supernaturals, they'll let us pass."

"Good plan," Noah said. Then he returned his attention to me. "Can you keep driving and hold one hand out so I can put this on you?"

I removed one hand from the wheel and held it out to the side, focusing on using my other hand to keep steady as I drove.

Noah took my hand, his skin warm against mine, and gently slid the ring onto my finger. I wasn't sure if I was imagining it or not, but it seemed like he let his fingers linger on my skin for a few seconds longer than necessary.

His touch was far more distracting than the shifter gangsters surrounding us, threatening to turn us into a midnight snack.

Once the ring was secure, I moved my hand back to the wheel. I had to keep my eyes on the road and not to look over at Noah.

I couldn't afford any distractions right now—especially those in the form of a sexy wolf shifter with a hidden past whose heart could never be mine.

"Keep driving," Sage said. "I'm going to roll down the window again and try to talk to them."

She did as she said, wind rushing through the car once the window was down. "We're shifters, just like you," she said to the men driving next to us. "Let us go on our way. We don't want any trouble."

The men said nothing in return. They simply howled, laughing as they did so. The others in the cars surrounding us all leaned out their windows and howled as well. It was eerie—like a hunting call—and I felt like a trapped animal.

Suddenly, the trucks on both sides of me moved closer and closer, until they were inches away from the Range Rover. A ripping, shredding sound screeched through the air.

Our tires. They'd slashed our tires.

The Rover wobbled. I tried to control it, but it was hopeless.

The coyotes' trucks moved out of the way just as I lost control of the car and went spinning out into the desert.

43

RAVEN

WE CAME to a stop in the sandy brush. I pressed down on the gas pedal again, but it was useless—the tires were destroyed.

The trucks were all much further along down the freeway, but they were turning around, coming for us. With the Rover stuck, we were sitting ducks.

"They're looking for a fight," Noah said. "And there are six of them and two of us."

"*Three* of us," I corrected him.

"Two of us who are able to fight." He glared at me, as if daring me to contradict him.

Sage reached into the potions bag and removed four deep purple pods. The memory potion. She handed two to Noah and kept two for herself.

"Their windows are all down so they can howl and

attempt to intimidate us, so throw one of these into the cab of each truck," she told him. "It'll release enough for both of them inside to breathe in. Tell them that there were only two of us in the Range Rover—not three. And you," she said, turning to me. "Get back here, put the blanket over you, and *stay down* and *stay quiet*. We'll come get you once it's safe. Got it?"

The headlights on the trucks were getting closer. The coyotes still howled, their eerie calls echoing through the desert.

If Noah and Sage were humans who could shift into wolves, these creepy men seemed more like coyotes that could shift into humans. More animalistic than human.

It wouldn't be long until they pulled off the freeway to join us. And given that they'd destroyed our tires *after* learning that Sage was a shifter, I knew they were trouble.

I wanted to insist on helping them fight. But I also wasn't stupid. Noah and Sage needed to focus on fighting the coyotes—not on protecting me. And once the coyotes shifted, it'd take only one of them to rip me to shreds in a minute.

So I did as Sage said and climbed into the back.

"On the floor," she said. "They won't see you there."

"What happens if you don't win?" I asked as I situated myself on the floor of the backseat. It was squished, but I managed.

"We've faced much worse than a pack of hungry coyotes," Noah said confidently. "Don't worry. We'll win."

I heard the sound of trucks surrounding us. They were here.

Noah pulled the blanket over me so it covered me completely, entrenching me in darkness. "With Sage's ring on, they won't be able to smell that you're here." He gave my shoulder a small squeeze, as if trying to reassure me. "You're safe."

The doors opened, and Noah and Sage stepped out of the Rover. They must have moved fast with the memory potion bombs, because I heard coughing and both of their voices as they told our ambushers the lie Sage had created—that they were the only two who had been in the car.

I held my breath and crossed my fingers, hoping it worked.

If it didn't, it wouldn't be long until one of the coyotes burst into the car and turned me into dinner.

Just in case that happened, I reached for the knife in my boot. Realistically, I knew it wouldn't save me against a supernatural coyote shifter. But if attacked, I refused to go down without a fight.

Truck doors slammed open and shut, and I heard the ploofing sounds as the men got out of their trucks.

"Just the wolf shifter we were looking for," one of them said with what sounded like a grin.

"You slashed our tires." Sage sounded *pissed*. "Why?"

"Are you both shifters?" He didn't answer her question. "Because I can't smell anything from you—not supernatural *or* human."

I assumed he was talking to Noah, since he was still wearing his ring.

"I'm a wolf shifter too," Noah said. "And trust me when I say that you don't want to mess with me—with either of us. Not if you know what's good for you."

"That's a powerful concealment charm you've got on you," another creepy male said. "Worth a pretty penny."

"Try to take it and you're dead." Noah sounded calm —lethal.

"Do you have any idea what's happening in the world?" Sage interrupted, clearly trying to get their attention away from Noah's ring. "About the demons that escaped from Hell? The ones who want to kill all supernaturals, turn the humans into slaves, and claim Earth as their own?"

"I've heard a thing or two." The man chuckled. "But I ain't seen no demons around these parts."

"You haven't seen them *yet*," Noah said. "But they'll come for you. Eventually."

"If they're coming for us, then they're coming for you, too." The man laughed again. "And I don't like your attitude, boy. Why you acting like you're so special? Like you're better than us?"

I could hear the challenge in his tone—like he was aching for a fight.

"I'm hunting demons," Noah said. "Killed six so far. I have the teeth to prove it. The more I kill, the safer we'll be. *All* of us."

"We ain't trying to stop you." The man coughed and spit out what sounded like a massive loogie. I nearly gagged in disgust. "We just want the girl."

"What girl?" Noah sounded tense—on edge. Like he was ready to shift and kill at a moment's notice.

Was the man talking about me? Did the memory potion not work? Did he know I was here?

I held my breath, afraid that even the smallest sound could give me away.

"Are you blind and stupid, boy?" The man spit again. "I'm talkin' bout that pretty girl right next to you. Sage Montgomery."

I could breathe again with the realization that they didn't know I was here.

"How do you know my name?" Sage asked.

"Just come with us, sweetheart," he said. "Be real nice and cooperate, and we might even let your lover boy here live."

"Cooperate?" Disbelief filled Sage's tone. "You shredded my tires, drove me off the road, cornered me at night in the middle of nowhere, threatened my hunting partner... and you think I'm going to *cooperate?*" She laughed at the ridiculousness of it all. "If you're being serious, then you've clearly never met a Montgomery."

There was a scuffle, and I heard howls and snarls from outside. The howls no longer sounded human. They were louder and deeper, sounding like they came from the throats of angry animals.

They all must have shifted.

The fight had begun.

44

RAVEN

I HEARD THE GROWLS, yips, bangs, and whimpers as the shifters launched at each other and attacked. My stomach twisted with nerves for Noah and Sage. I know they'd said they were confident they would win, but this was six against two. And those coyotes seemed pretty feral.

But I'd watched them defeat a *demon*. I'd seen the six demon teeth Noah carried in his pocket—evidence of the demons he'd killed. Surely if they could beat demons, they could beat coyotes?

I kept telling myself that was the case. But the fight continued on. I didn't know how long it had been—it felt like forever. Shouldn't they be done by now? It had taken Noah *seconds* to overtake that demon—Eli—in the alley.

I heard an anguished howl, followed by a pitiful whimper. Someone was hurt.

Could it be Noah or Sage? I had no way to distinguish between the sounds of the coyotes and the wolves. I'd only be able to tell if I could look.

I needed to check and make sure they were okay. But they'd been clear earlier. I needed to stay hidden under the blanket, so the coyotes didn't see me.

I hated this. My friends—the people who had saved my life and were now helping me save my mom's life— could be in danger. No—they *were* in danger. Because if they were truly able to defeat the coyotes as easily as they'd claimed, this fight would have been over by now.

And I was hiding in the car, doing nothing.

A helpless, useless human.

Except that I wasn't totally useless. Because Sage had given me a knife… and she'd taught me about potions. And here I was, hiding out with the bag full of potions right in front of my face.

Potions were defensive—not offensive—but there had to be one of them for me to use.

I ran through all the potions she'd taught me about during our drive, excitement sparking in my chest when I realized which one was *perfect* for my current situation.

As quietly as possible, I unzipped the bag, keeping

the blanket over me and the bag like a tent while doing so. Some potions had a dim glow to them, and I couldn't risk the light being seen through the windows of the car. As it was, the fight outside was *loud*, so I hoped it covered up any small sounds I might be making.

It didn't take much digging to find the clear potion I was searching for. It looked like water. It was in a small vial, since it was one of the potions that only worked when ingested.

I popped off the rubber top and eyed up the potion.

Did I *really* want to do this? Noah and Sage had told me how expensive potions were. They were at least a thousand bucks a dose—and those were the cheap ones. That was why they only used them when necessary.

I wasn't sure if this qualified as necessary. And who knew when they'd be able to replace it next?

A deep snarl and another anguished howl filled the night. Someone was in pain.

Was it Noah? Or Sage? Not knowing what was going on out there was driving me crazy. Plus, it seemed like the Montgomery pack had enough money that a thousand bucks wasn't a huge deal to them. So… bottoms up.

I raised the vial to my lips and downed it like a shot.

It tasted like nothing. Literally, *water* was flavorful in comparison. This was like drinking air.

For a moment I thought it wasn't going to work. But

then an icy coldness traveled through my veins, starting at my center and spreading out to my fingers and toes.

When I held my hand in front of me, it was transparent. Like a ghost. Everything I was wearing at the time of drinking the potion was transparent, too.

I could see myself. But according to what Sage had told me earlier, no one else would be able to—at least for the next hour, which was how long the potion would continue working.

Because I was invisible.

RAVEN

SINCE I'D BEEN WRAPPED in the blanket while taking the potion, it had turned invisible too. I threw it off me, since I wouldn't need it anymore, and got up to look out the window.

I gasped at the scene before me, shock and fear clawing my heart.

Noah was fighting a mountain lion. And judging by how the lion kept lunging and Noah kept dodging, he wasn't winning.

At least, I assumed that the brown wolf with the white underbelly was Noah. The brown was the same color as his hair. The other wolf—the one I assumed was Sage—was smaller, with black fur. She was holding off three coyotes of her own. The coyotes were smaller than she was, but they were quick and vicious guerrilla warriors as they went in for their attacks.

The other two coyotes were dead, beheaded and splayed out on the ground in puddles of their own blood.

The lion pawed at Noah, but he avoided its sharp claws every time. Noah was agile and fast, but his breaths were deep—labored. I feared he wouldn't be able to keep this up for much longer. And while shifters could heal, if their brains or hearts got punctured, there was no coming back from that.

He needed Sage's help. But one of the coyotes Sage was fighting went for her leg, another catching her tail. She snapped her teeth and howled. All the while, Noah was slowly losing speed against the lion's attacks.

That was it. I couldn't sit here and watch my friends get slaughtered. I might not have supernatural strength, but with both my appearance and scent hidden, I had the element of surprise on my side. And I intended on using it.

I reached for my boot knife—it was invisible too, since it had been on me when I'd taken the potion. Knife in hand, I crawled across the seat and opened the door that wasn't in the line of sight of the fight. I hopped out, not closing the door. I couldn't risk the sound of it slamming shut calling attention to the fact that I was here.

I moved as quickly as possible, avoiding stepping on the patches of brush. The shifters were all involved in their fights, but the tiny bushes being crushed under an invisible foot would be an obvious giveaway of my location. The fact that I was leaving footsteps in the dirt was already risky enough.

I hurried toward where Sage fought the coyotes. She was already mostly healed from the previous attack I'd witnessed. But the same two coyotes circled directly around her with supernatural speed and kept nipping at her legs, faster than she had time to recover. She snapped at their throats, although she missed.

She was losing steam.

The third coyote jogged around them, watching them with intensity. It appeared to be keeping her away from where Noah was fighting the lion.

I sneaked up behind the third coyote, sliding my knife straight through its neck and up into its brain. It gave a small yip and collapsed to the ground.

The coyotes circling Sage turned at the distraction.

She used the moment of advantage to capture one of their necks in her jaw, snap its head clean off, and fling its lifeless body to the ground. The final coyote's beheaded corpse was seconds behind.

Sage ran straight at me, using her nose to nudge the

knife from my hand. It clattered to the ground between us.

How did she know I was standing there?

The coyote's blood, I realized. *The knife was invisible, since I was wearing it when I drank the potion. But the blood coating the knife wasn't. Sage had pushed it out of my hand because she didn't want me to give away my location.*

I didn't have time to thank her before she turned to help Noah.

Jaws open, she ran for the lion's underbelly, catapulting forward and knocking the beast on its side. Blood spurted from its stomach in droves. She must have hit a vein. It took all of my self-control not to jump up and cheer her on.

Noah was on top of the lion in a second, his jaws clamped around its neck. I heard a sickeningly loud crunch as he broke its spine, and the rip of flesh as he tore its head off its body.

The mountain lion was dead.

And from the look Noah was shooting in my general direction—his lips curled back to reveal the lion's blood still on his teeth—he looked like he wanted to kill me next.

46

RAVEN

NOAH AND SAGE shifted back to their human forms. Whatever injuries they'd gotten during the fight had already healed. And their clothes remained on. I supposed shifters were able to shift with their clothes, the same way that everything I was wearing also turned invisible when I'd taken the potion. That was handy, since the other option—them being naked after shifting —would have been pretty awkward.

"Raven." Noah stepped over the mountain lion's corpse, his eyes narrowed in my general direction. "What the *hell* were you thinking?"

"You can see me?" I was so surprised that he knew where I was that I ignored his question.

"I can't see you," he said. "Since clearly, you took the

liberty of helping yourself to our invisibility potion. But I can smell you."

"How?" I held up my hand—the one wearing Sage's ring. "I'm cloaked."

"The rings that Sage and I have were forged from the same stone and created under the same spell." He crossed his arms, as if I should understand the implication of what that meant. "They're linked."

"Those wearing linked rings will be able to sense each other, even though no one else will be able to sense them," Sage added. "It's useful while hunting, since it's important to be able to sense your partner. So right now, Noah can sense you, and if you were a supernatural, you'd be able to sense him. I can't sense either of you, since you're wearing my ring and Noah's wearing his."

"Okay," I said. "Got it."

"I can't talk to you like this." Noah growled, gesturing in my general direction. "Sage, get her an antidote pill from the car."

"I can get my own antidote pill." I placed my bloodied knife back inside my boot and marched to the car, not wanting anyone to have to fetch anything for me.

"It's in the front pocket of the bag!" Sage called out. "The pink ones. They're chewable."

As I made my way to the Range Rover, I realized how strange this situation would look to any passing outsider. Five cars pulled over to the side of the freeway past midnight, their headlights illuminating three people standing amongst the freshly beheaded corpses of coyotes and a mountain lion.

It was a good thing no one was driving this far out in the middle of nowhere at this time of night.

Well, no one except for us. Which, judging how well *that* had gone, had been a pretty stupid move.

It didn't take long for me to find the pink pills—they were where Sage had said, in a zip locked baggie in the front. The antidote pills had been something else that Sage had told me about during our long drive. They could counter the effect of most potions, but only when the pill had been created by the same witch who had brewed the potion. In this case, both the pill and potion had been created by Whitney—Amber's sister who had been murdered by Azazel. The antidote would only work on potions brewed by Whitney.

Since Whitney was dead, we had to be careful with how many of the pills we used. Once they were gone, there would be no way to create an antidote to any of Whitney's remaining potions.

Given that the invisibility potion would have run out

of juice in less than an hour, Noah must have commanded I take the pill because he was *pissed*.

I popped the pill in my mouth, chewed, and swallowed. It coated my tongue like chalk. I imagined it was doing that to the rest of my body as well.

I held one of my hands up to my face, watching the ghost-like haze become more and more opaque, until I was visible again. The blanket that had turned invisible with me turned visible again as well.

When I stepped back around the car, Noah and Sage were bickering about something. Their conversation ceased when they saw me.

"Good." Noah nodded in approval and marched toward me, anger swirling in his eyes. "Now I can see your reaction when you tell me what the hell were you thinking by getting involved back there."

"I was thinking that you were fighting a mountain lion on your own, Sage was struggling against three coyotes, and that if I didn't do something to help, those shifters would have come for me next." I raised my chin, determined to stay strong and show no weakness. "I couldn't risk that happening."

"We were handling it," he said. "You would have been safer if you'd stayed put."

"Maybe," I said, since none of us knew what would

have happened if I hadn't stepped in. "But why didn't you tell me that one of them was a *mountain lion* shifter? I thought they were all coyotes."

"It was irrelevant." Noah's jaw tightened. "You were safe, and we were beating them. We had it covered."

"It didn't look like that from what I saw."

"You weren't supposed to *see* anything!" He motioned toward the Rover—the white car was covered in dust, looking a wreck with its destroyed tires. "You were supposed to stay hidden under that blanket."

"You told me the fight wouldn't take long," I said. "It was taking long. I was worried that something was wrong."

"Nothing was wrong." He growled and took another step forward, so there were only inches between us. "But how am I supposed to protect you when you do something stupid like that?" He looked like he wanted to reach for my shoulders and shake some sense into me, but he flexed his fists instead.

Now we both held each other's gazes. Neither of us said a word, and neither of us backed down. If he was trying to intimidate me, I refused to let him.

"We didn't know that one of the shifters was a mountain lion," Sage admitted, her voice barely louder than a whisper.

"What?" I whipped my head to face her—she was looking down at the ground in shame—and then I looked back to Noah. "You said you knew. You lied."

"I didn't lie." He shifted on his feet. "I never said we knew the shifter was a mountain lion. I just said that his being a mountain lion was irrelevant."

"Same thing," I muttered.

"No," he said. "It's not."

"Fine." I looked back and forth between the two of them. "But how did neither of you sense a *mountain lion*? And how did a mountain lion join up with a pack of coyotes, anyway?" I didn't know much about wild animals, but those two species didn't seem like the types to naturally mix. Sort of like dogs and cats... but bigger.

And supernatural.

My life had *seriously* taken a turn for the insane.

"It was cloaked," he said, motioning to his ring. "Like we are. We didn't know until it shifted into its coyote form... and *then* into a mountain lion."

"It was mated with a mountain lion," I realized. "So it could assume both forms."

"Correct," he said. "And also correct that mountain lions and coyotes wouldn't naturally mix. Coyotes—like wolves—are pack animals. Big cats like mountain lions tend to be more solitary."

"And more lethal." I eyed up the lion behind us, dread filling my stomach at what might have happened if I hadn't helped Sage with those coyotes so she could help Noah with the lion.

"It wasn't too bad." Noah sounded a bit too modest considering the fight I'd witnessed. "It's just a good thing it wasn't a tiger. Then we would have been in some serious trouble."

"A *tiger*?" I widened my eyes, catching my jaw before it dropped to the ground. "There are *tiger shifters*?"

"Oh yeah," Sage said. "They live in India—in the vampire kingdom of the Haven. They're the most deadly type of shifter out there. It would take an entire pack of wolves to even have a chance at taking down one tiger. I've never seen one, but Noah has."

"You've been to India?" I tilted my head as I looked up at him, surprised.

He raised an eyebrow. "Why does it sound like you find that crazier than the existence of tiger shifters?" he asked.

"I don't," I said, although I realized a second later that it wasn't totally the truth. "I just... well, I guess I just don't know much about your past, do I?"

"You don't." He lowered his voice, as if warning me not to push the subject any further.

"All right." I swallowed, suddenly eager to change the subject. "But no matter what you say, I *did* help you back there. I deserve at least an acknowledgment... or a thank you."

"You did help," Sage said. "I would have eventually fought off those coyotes on my own, but in time to help Noah against the mountain lion?" She shrugged and glanced back at the lion, doubt crossing her eyes. "I don't know."

I knew then that while my decision had been risky, it had been right. I'd do it all over again in a heartbeat.

"Just don't pull a stunt like that again," Noah said. "You got lucky this time, but don't push that luck. Not if you want to stay alive."

"Maybe it doesn't have to be luck." I straightened my shoulders in challenge. "Maybe you—both of you—could teach me how to fight."

"I thought you wanted to get to Avalon as quickly as possible?" he asked.

"I do." Obviously that hadn't changed, since the sooner I got to Avalon, the sooner I could save my mom.

"Then we don't have time to teach you how to fight," he said. "You trust us to keep you safe, and that's final."

I opened my mouth to protest, but he held a hand up to stop me.

"Now, which of these trucks should we hijack?" He took a good look at the old, rusted pick-up trucks that had belonged to the coyotes. "Because we sure as hell aren't making it to New Orleans on four shredded tires."

47

FLINT

I WALKED into the back room of the dimly lit bar, my veins thrumming with excitement when I spotted the beautiful blonde at the corner table nursing a drink. I'd felt her presence the moment I'd walked inside the building, but seeing her made my heart race in a way it never had before.

"Mara." I breathed her name as if it were life itself, joining her at the table.

She stood, wrapping her arms around my neck in a fluid motion as her lips joined mine. She smelled like a warm campfire on a winter night. It was the distinct scent of demon, but one I'd come to love, as I now associated it with her.

"Flint." She gazed up at me through her seductive red eyes—the eyes that had stolen a piece of my soul.

I recalled the first time I'd seen those eyes, when I'd walked into this bar last week. I'd been repulsed to find a demon frequenting my favorite bar in the city. I'd marched up to her and grabbed her, ready to tell her she wasn't welcome and to order her to leave.

The moment my hands had wrapped around her wrists, I'd felt an undeniable pull toward her. I'd wanted her. Then, when our lips met for the first time, it was like strings bringing our souls together. I'd *felt* her, and what I felt wasn't evil.

It was the soul of a beautiful woman who had finally escaped her desolate home and was ready to make a new home for herself on Earth.

I knew at once that I wanted to help her. Because the connection between us—the way my soul sang for hers —was undeniable.

I'd imprinted on her.

It was unheard of for a shifter to imprint outside of our species, but it had happened. And it had happened both ways. She hadn't realized what it was at first, since imprinting was an experience unique to shifters, but she'd imprinted on me as well.

I believed it had happened for a reason—so that Mara and I could mate, allowing me to provide safety to my pack in these dark times to come.

"I spoke with Azazel." She smiled as she sat back down, and I sat with her, anticipating good news. Her hands didn't let go of mine, and I squeezed them tighter.

I would never let her go.

"And?" I leaned forward, eager for her to continue.

"Once your pack completes the blood binding spell that swears your allegiance to him, he will allow us to mate."

I drew her toward me, kissing her again. Actions always spoke for me when words failed.

"I take it you're happy?" she asked once we broke apart, her eyes shining as they gazed up into mine.

"That's an understatement." I cupped her delicate features with my hand, thrilled that this beautiful woman would officially be mine. "This is the way everything's supposed to be."

"It is," she agreed. "But Azazel isn't known for his patience. When will your pack be ready for the ceremony?"

"The moment my sister returns," I told her.

"And when will that be?"

"Soon," I promised. "I contacted some allies of mine and offered them a substantial monetary reward if they fetched her as she drove by their territory. They should be bringing her back as we speak."

"*Should?*" She raised an eyebrow. "Have you received confirmation from these allies of yours?"

"They're on it." I puffed out my chest, annoyed that she doubted me. But of course, one look into her soulful eyes stopped me from being annoyed for long. "According to the tracking device I had installed on her phone, they pulled her over right before I came in here. They'll bring her back home. Once she's returned, we'll commence the ceremony immediately."

I felt slightly guilty for sending the coyotes after Sage —my headstrong sister hated being told what to do, even by her alpha. She was far more connected to her humanity than I'd ever been. Still, I loved her, and I wouldn't leave her on her own. This was for her own good.

Because if she knew I was making a deal with the demons, she'd never voluntarily return.

After the blood binding with Azazel, Sage would come to her senses and forgive me for abducting her and ordering my allies to kill Noah and the redheaded human. After all, I couldn't risk Noah and the human following her. Pack was *always* first, and they weren't pack.

My sister would forgive me because the connection with the greater demon would overpower her humanity for good.

It was best this way. The path had been clear from the moment I'd imprinted with Mara.

Because once the blood binding alliance with Azazel was complete, the demons would no longer be a threat to us.

It was the only way for me to make sure the Montgomery pack—*my* pack—would be safe in the dark times to come.

I hope you enjoyed The Angel Trials! If so, I'd love if you left a review. Reviews help readers find the book, and I read each and every one of them :)

Here's the link on Amazon where you can leave your review ➜ The Angel Trials

---

The next book in the series, The Angel Hunt, is out now!

Get your copy now at:
mybook.to/angelhunt

You can also check out the cover and description for

The Angel Hunt below. (You may need to turn the page to view the cover and description.)

The hunt for demons is about to heat up.

Somehow Raven has convinced Noah and Sage—the two wolf shifters who saved her from a demon attack—to let her tag along on their quest to kill ten demons. The payoff for completing the mission? Entrance to the mystical island of Avalon, where Raven will go through trials to gain the strength she needs to save her mom's life.

Raven wants to help the shifters on their quest. But Noah refuses to put her in any danger—which makes no sense, since he hates her. At least she *thinks* he hates her… until he catches her off guard and kisses her.

Suddenly they're connected in ways she doesn't understand, and she feels closer to him than ever.

If she didn't know any better, she'd think they imprinted on each other. But that's impossible. Because shifters can't imprint on humans.

And if they *did* imprint on each other, then the supernatural world is changing—and Raven's right in the center of it.

Emotions will flare between Raven and Noah in the second book in The Angel Trials series, an urban fantasy adventure with romance, magic, and twists that will keep you reading long into the night!

Get your copy now at:
mybook.to/angelhunt

Also, make sure you never miss a new release by signing up to get emails and/or texts when my books come out!

Sign up for emails: michellemadow.com/subscribe

Sign up for texts: michellemadow.com/texts

And if you want to hang out with me and other readers of my books, make sure to join my Facebook group: www.facebook.com/groups/michellemadow

Thanks for reading my books, and I look forward to chatting with you!

ABOUT THE AUTHOR

Michelle Madow is a USA Today bestselling author of fast-paced fantasy novels that will leave you turning the pages wanting more! Her books are full of magic, adventure, romance, and twists you'll never see coming.

Michelle grew up in Maryland, and now lives in Florida. She's loved reading for as long as she can remember. She wrote her first book in her junior year of college and hasn't stopped writing since! She also loves traveling, and has been to all seven continents. Someday, she hopes to travel the world for a year on a cruise ship.

Visit author.to/MichelleMadow to view a full list of Michelle's novels on Amazon.

THE ANGEL TRIALS

Published by Dreamscape Publishing

Copyright © 2018 Michelle Madow

ASIN: B079K6G8ZP

❀ Created with Vellum

Made in the USA
Middletown, DE
20 May 2022

65996733R00163